THE MYSTERY AT
The Ski Jump

Books by

CAROLYN KEENE

Nancy Drew Mystery Stories

The Secret of the Old Clock
The Hidden Staircase
The Bungalow Mystery
The Mystery at Lilac Inn
The Secret at Shadow Ranch
The Secret of Red Gate Farm
The Clue in the Diary
Nancy's Mysterious Letter
The Sign of the Twisted Candles
The Password to Larkspur Lane
The Clue of the Broken Locket
The Message in the Hollow Oak
The Mystery of the Ivory Charm
The Whispering Statue
The Haunted Bridge
The Clue of the Tapping Heels
The Mystery of the Brass Bound
Trunk

The Mystery at the Moss-Covered
Mansion
The Quest of the Missing Map
The Clue in the Jewel Box
The Secret in the Old Attic
The Clue in the Crumbling Wall
The Mystery of the Tolling Bell
The Clue in the Old Album
The Ghost of Blackwood Hall
The Clue of the Leaning Chimney
The Secret of the Wooden Lady
The Clue of the Black Keys
The Mystery at the Ski Jump
The Clue of the Velvet Mask
The Ringmaster's Secret
The Scarlet Slipper Mystery
The Witch Tree Symbol
The Hidden Window Mystery

The Haunted Showboat

Dana Girls Mystery Stories

By the Light of the Study Lamp
The Secret at Lone Tree Cottage
In the Shadow of the Tower
A Three-Cornered Mystery
The Secret at the Hermitage
The Circle of Footprints
The Mystery of the Locked Room
The Clue in the Cobweb
The Secret at the Gatehouse
The Mysterious Fireplace

The Clue of the Rusty Key
The Portrait in the Sand
The Secret in the Old Well
The Clue in the Ivy
The Secret of the Jade Ring
Mystery at the Crossroads
The Ghost in the Gallery
The Clue of the Black Flower
The Winking Ruby Mystery
The Secret of the Swiss Chalet

Crying loudly for help, Nancy dashed off in pursuit of the thief.

NANCY DREW MYSTERY STORIES

THE MYSTERY AT
The Ski Jump

BY CAROLYN KEENE

NEW YORK

Grosset & Dunlap

PUBLISHERS

Contents

THE MYSTERY AT
The Ski Jump

CHAPTER I

The Strange Woman

"BRR—R, it's cold!"

Nancy Drew shivered and pulled the collar of her scarlet coat higher against the driving snow. Determinedly, she ducked her head and pushed along the darkening street.

Suddenly, out of nowhere, a long, black car skidded across the sidewalk directly in front of her.

"Oh!" Nancy cried out, leaping back just in time to keep from being hit. A second later the car crashed into a porch.

As Nancy dashed forward to see if the driver were hurt, the door of the house flew open and the excited owner, Mrs. Martin, rushed out.

"What happened?" she demanded. Seeing the car, Mrs. Martin ran down the snowy steps. "Is someone hurt?"

Nancy was already twisting at the handle of the

driver's door.   When she yanked it open they saw a slender woman in a fur coat slumped across the steering wheel.   Together they carried the unconscious stranger into the house and laid her on a couch in the living room.

"I think she's only stunned," Nancy announced, pressing her fingers to the victim's wrist.   "Her pulse is regular and the color's coming back to her cheeks."

"Just the same, I think we ought to call Dr. Britt," Mrs. Martin said nervously.   "Will you do it, Nancy?   The phone's in the hall.   I'll get a blanket to put over her."

Nancy called Dr. Britt's office.   The line was busy and it was nearly five minutes before she could get a connection.

"Dr. Britt is out," she reported to Mrs. Martin, as the woman came down the stairs with a blanket. "His nurse said she would telephone him and ask the doctor to stop here as soon as possible."

"*Doctor!* Who wants a doctor?" called an annoyed voice from the living room.   "I have no need for a doctor."

Nancy and Mrs. Martin were amazed to see the woman from the car sitting up on the couch.   She was removing a gold make-up kit from the pocket of her coat.   Now she calmly began to powder her nose, and dab on some exotic perfume.

Nancy appraised her quickly—a strikingly

handsome woman about thirty-five, with blue-black hair, pale skin, and high cheekbones. An expensive mink coat was draped nonchalantly over her slim shoulders.

"Why, Mrs. Channing," said Mrs. Martin suddenly, "I didn't recognize you at first. I'm glad you feel better. Nancy, Mrs. Channing is from the Forest Fur Company.

"Mrs. Channing, I'd like you to meet Nancy Drew. She lives here in River Heights with her father—he's a famous lawyer. And Nancy's one of the best young detectives I ever—"

"Lawyer—detective!" Mrs. Channing interrupted. There was such a sharp expression in her dark-blue eyes when she looked at Nancy that the girl felt slightly embarrassed.

"At least Dad is a fine lawyer," she replied, smiling. "Sometimes he asks me to help him on his cases. Your work must be interesting, too, Mrs. Channing. I've never heard of the Forest Fur Company. Where is it?"

"Oh, we have many branches, Miss Drew. All over the country."

Mrs. Channing started to rise from the sofa but fell back weakly.

"I think you really should see a doctor," Nancy suggested kindly. "You're still shaky from the accident."

"I'll be all right!" Mrs. Channing answered

emphatically. "Perhaps if I have a cup of tea—"

Nancy turned to Mrs. Martin. "I think I'd better run along," she said.

"Oh, it's so cold outside, do stay and have a cup of tea with us. It won't take a minute."

"Thank you, but I really can't," Nancy replied. "I'm leaving with Dad on a trip in the morning and have a lot of last-minute packing to do."

Nancy was looking forward to helping her father on a case in Montreal. He had promised to tell her about it at dinner.

A few minutes later she was shaking the snow from her coat and boots on the back porch of the Drew home. Opening the kitchen door, she called:

"Hello, Mrs. Gruen. I'm back."

"Well, I'm certainly relieved," replied a motherly voice from the hall. "What a storm!"

The Drews' middle-aged housekeeper walked into the kitchen and smiled affectionately at Nancy. Hannah Gruen had been with the family for several years—ever since Nancy's mother had passed away.

"I was delayed by an accident," Nancy explained. "Car jumped the curb. The driver wasn't hurt, but I'm afraid Mrs. Martin's porch will need a lot of repairing."

The conversation was interrupted by a telephone call from Nancy's friend, Ned Nickerson, asking for a date to a fraternity dance next month. She accepted gaily, then went upstairs to start packing. Five minutes later Hannah hustled into the bedroom.

"Look what I have to show you!" cried the housekeeper.

Nancy's eyes danced. "A mink scarf!" she exclaimed. "It's beautiful!"

"It was *such* a bargain, I couldn't resist it," Mrs. Gruen explained excitedly. "I've always wanted a fur scarf but dared not spend the money."

Nancy took the lovely neckpiece and laid it around her shoulders.

"It's a gorgeous scarf," she said. "Where did you buy it?"

"From a *very* charming lady," Mrs. Gruen answered. "She was from the Forest Fur Company. You see, she had already sold a scarf to my friend, Esther Mills. And Esther suggested—"

Nancy was not listening. At mention of the Forest Fur Company her thoughts went racing back to the mysterious Mrs. Channing.

"Nancy, do you think I was foolish?" the housekeeper asked as the girl frowned.

"I—I'm not sure," Nancy answered absently. "It does look like a good fur piece. But it's an odd way to sell expensive furs."

"I hope everything's all right," said Hannah, a worried look replacing her former eagerness. "I also invested some money in Forest Fur Company stock. The lady, a Mrs. Channing, sold me ten shares. I gave her fifty dollars for it. But I'm sure it's okay. I have the certificate in my bureau drawer."

"Where is she staying?" Nancy asked.

"Why, I don't know. She didn't tell me."

At that moment Nancy heard the front door close and the sound of her father's firm footsteps in the hall. She laid an arm about Mrs. Gruen's plump shoulders and gave her a comforting squeeze.

"Don't worry. I'll run down and talk this over with Dad," she assured the housekeeper. "Perhaps he knows the Forest Fur Company."

"Dad!" called Nancy, reaching the bottom step. "I'm so glad you're home."

"Hello, dear." Tall, handsome Carson Drew kissed her cheek. "Say, do I detect a worried look in those pretty blue eyes?"

"Well, something's on my mind," Nancy acknowledged, and told her father about Mrs. Channing and the Forest Fur Company.

"I've never heard of the company," the lawyer remarked when she finished. "But I certainly don't like the way they do business. No reliable company would peddle expensive furs and stock from door to door at bargain prices. Please ask Hannah to let me see her certificate."

After reading it, he had to admit it looked all right, but added that he thought the company should be investigated.

"Mrs. Channing is still at Mrs. Martin's," Nancy said excitedly. "Suppose I go over there and talk to her."

"Fine," Carson Drew nodded. "I'll go with you. We can't let our Hannah be taken in by swindlers."

The Martin home was only two blocks away. As the Drews reached it, Nancy cried out that Mrs. Channing's car was gone. She dashed up the broken porch steps and rang the bell hurriedly. The door swung open.

"Mrs. Martin, is Mrs. Channing—?" Nancy began.

"She's gone!"

"In her car?"

Mrs. Martin's eyes blazed. "Yes. To put it plainly, Nancy, Mrs. Channing ran out on me. When I brought that tea she asked for, she was gone! Her car too! And not one word did she say about paying for the damage she did to my porch!"

"What's her address?" Nancy asked quickly.

Mrs. Martin stared vacantly. "I don't know."

CHAPTER II

A Serious Loss

MRS. MARTIN invited Nancy and her father into the house and offered them chairs before the crackling fire.

"I suppose I'll never find that Mrs. R. I. Channing!" she sputtered. "But that Forest Fur Company will pay for repairing my porch! Don't you think they should, Mr. Drew?"

"That depends on whether or not Mrs. Channing was using a car of theirs, or at least was doing business for them at the time of the accident. Suppose you tell us everything you know about this woman."

Before Mrs. Martin could start, they heard the sound of heavy feet on the porch stomping off snow, followed by the sound of the door buzzer. The caller was Dr. Britt, tired and cold after his long drive through the storm. When he learned that his intended patient had left in such a rude way, the physician was indignant.

"I don't blame you for being angry, Mrs. Martin," he agreed, stepping into the living room. "Anyone as ungrateful as Mrs. Channing doesn't deserve sympathy. Good evening, Mr. Drew. Hello, Nancy."

Mrs. Martin indicated a third chair facing the fire. "You sit here and rest, Doctor," she urged. "I was just going to tell what I know about Mrs. Channing.

"She came here two days ago and sold me a mink scarf and some stock in a fur company. She promised that the stock would make me a great deal of money. But now I don't trust her. You know what I think? That she ran away from here because of you, Nancy."

"What!"

"Before I went to get the tea," Mrs. Martin explained, "I told her how many cases you solved yourself—not just for your father. Like *The Clue of the Black Keys* and *The Secret of the Wooden Lady*. Now that I think of it, I believe Mrs. Channing got scared and left. We'll never find her."

"Mrs. Channing also sold a mink scarf and some stock to our housekeeper, Mrs. Gruen," volunteered Nancy. "That's why I came back here."

Dr. Britt looked thoughtful. *"Channing . . .*

Channing!" he murmured. "I thought that name sounded familiar. Now I remember. My nurse, Ida Compton, showed me a fur piece and some stock certificates she purchased from a woman named Channing."

"This is very interesting," Mr. Drew spoke up. "Nancy, why don't you see Miss Compton and find out if she can give you some additional information about Mrs. Channing?"

"I certainly will," his daughter replied. "But by the time we get back from Montreal—"

"I'd suggest that you stay here a couple of days and see what you can find out," her father said. "You can follow me later."

He arose, adding that Hannah Gruen probably was becoming uneasy over their absence. She would want to know what they had learned about Mrs. Channing.

"And the delicious dinner I smelled will be spoiled." Nancy smiled.

"Let me drive you," offered the doctor. "Fortunately the storm is dying down. It should be fair by morning."

When the Drews arrived home, Mrs. Gruen met them with questioning eyes. They told her the truth but begged her not to worry about the fur company stock.

"It may be a good investment," said the lawyer cheerfully, although he doubted it. "And now, how about some food? This is the best eating place in the country, Hannah."

The housekeeper beamed. "Tonight it's pot roast and big browned potatoes exactly as you like them."

"Dessert?"

"Pie—your favorite. Apples with lots of cinnamon." Mrs. Gruen turned to Nancy. "Bess Marvin telephoned. She's coming over after dinner. And George—I never can get used to a girl with a boy's name—she's coming too."

"Grand!" said Nancy. "The three of us will hold a farewell party for you, Dad."

Bess and her cousin George Fayne arrived at eight o'clock. Clad in boots and woolen ski suits, they were in the highest spirits in spite of the cold. George, a trim boyish-looking girl with short, black hair and an independent swing to her shoulders, was the first through the door.

"Hypers! Isn't this storm something?" she exclaimed. "Old Man Winter is certainly doing his best to blow our town off the map," she panted. "One more big puff and I'd probably have landed on top a church steeple."

Bess giggled. "That would be something—you flapping about like a weathervane!"

"Bet I could point in all directions at once," George retorted.

"Well, I'd rather stay inside," said Bess, blond

and pretty. "Maybe we can make some fudge," she added hopefully. Bess loved sweets and worried little about her weight.

"I'm afraid there won't be time for cooking," said Nancy. "The fact is, I have some work for both of you."

"Nancy! You don't mean you're on the trail of another mystery?" George asked eagerly.

"Could be," Nancy answered, her eyes twinkling. For the next few minutes she explained to her friends about Mrs. R. I. Channing and her questionable method of selling stock and furs.

"I've just been examining the stock certificate she gave Mrs. Gruen," the young detective went on. "It gives the headquarters of the Forest Fur Company as Dunstan Lake, Vermont. But, girls, I've looked in the atlas and there's no such place as Dunstan Lake, Vermont."

"Too small, maybe?" George suggested.

"Dad has a directory like those used in the post office," Nancy went on. "It's not in there, either."

"Then it must be a phony outfit!" gasped Bess.

"Perhaps," agreed Nancy. "Anyway, I must find that Mrs. Channing as soon as possible. The roads are blocked by snow and she can't get far."

"We'll help you search," said George eagerly. "Just give the orders!"

"Okay." Nancy grinned. "Suppose you two call all the garages in town and see if anyone brought in a long, black car with damaged front fenders. Meanwhile, I'll use the private phone in Dad's study and call the local inns, hotels, tourist homes, and motor camps to see if a Mrs. Channing is registered."

When the girls met again twenty minutes later, all of them admitted complete failure. Because of the weather, Bess and George were sure Mrs. Channing could not have driven far. She probably had stayed with a friend.

"Unless she registered at a hotel under another name," Nancy mused.

Mr. Drew joined them in a "going-away" snack, then kissed Nancy good night. He told her he would be gone before she was awake, then asked:

"What's your next move?"

"To call on Ida Compton."

The next morning was crisp and sunny. Giant snowplows, working all night, had effectively cleared the highways. At ten o'clock the three girls were seated in Nancy's smart little convertible, on their way to consult the nurse. Nancy pulled up at Dr. Britt's home.

After hearing the story, Miss Compton was eager to co-operate. She explained that a few days previously, a tall, muscular man of about forty and his wife had called to see the doctor. They had given their names as Mr. and Mrs. R. I. Channing.

While they waited to see the doctor, the nurse expressed her admiration for the mink stole Mrs. Channing wore. To her surprise, the woman removed the scarf and offered to sell it cheap. She also offered Miss Compton a block of Forest Fur Company stock.

"Mrs. Channing doesn't miss a trick, does she?" George snorted. "Always on the lookout for clients!"

"Mrs. Channing *seemed* pleasant and honest," sighed the nurse. "Are you sure she isn't?"

"Well, I haven't *proved* anything yet," Nancy admitted. "But Mrs. Channing's methods are very strange, and I couldn't locate Dunstan Lake."

Miss Compton said she never left the office when strangers were in it. But at Mr. Channing's request she had gone to make a cup of tea because his wife felt faint.

"I'm afraid the tea business was just an excuse," Nancy said. "Those two wanted you out of here for some special reason. But why?"

The young detective's glance passed swiftly about the room and came to rest on a steel cabinet. "Of course!" she exclaimed. "The Channings wanted to look into the file. They wanted names and addresses of persons they might sell to."

"I guess that's true, Nancy," the nurse admitted. "Because as soon as Mrs. Channing drank the tea and I handed her a check for the scarf and the stock, she said they couldn't wait to see the doctor and hurried away."

"Miss Compton, will you do me a favor?" Nancy asked. "Call a few of the doctor's patients on the telephone right now. Ask if a Mrs. Channing, or at least a brunette woman, has called on them, offering to sell them stock or furs."

She had no sooner made her request than the nurse began to dial a number. Within a few minutes Nancy learned that several patients had made purchases from a smooth-tongued woman named Mrs. Channing. Nancy spoke to each one but picked up no further information.

"I think we had better be on our way," she said finally. "I don't want to take any more of your time, Miss Compton. But if you will continue to check the people in those files, we can stop in later for the list. *Somewhere* there's bound to be *someone* who can give us a real clue."

"Where do we go from here?" George asked, as the three friends piled back into the convertible.

"I don't know," said Nancy. "It's too near lunchtime to make any calls and—"

"*Girls!*"

Nancy's voice was excited as she bent over the steering wheel and stared down the street. "There! Just crossing the street in that car," she gasped. "I believe it's Mrs. Channing!"

As soon as the light changed, Nancy turned left

to follow the black car. She trailed it down the side street a block, then onto a highway that led to open country. All at once the girls' ears caught the warning wail of a siren. A police car drew up alongside the convertible. The driver waved Nancy to the curb.

"Where do you think you're going in such a hurry?" the officer demanded.

"Oh!" Nancy flushed. "I'm sorry if I was going too fast. You see there was another car—a car we had to catch up to."

The policeman ignored her apology. "Let's see your driver's license."

"Certainly, Officer."

Nancy reached for the wallet in her inner coat pocket. She snapped open its secret flap and suddenly her face was the picture of dismay.

Her driver's license and all her other identification cards were gone!

CHAPTER III

Missing Diamonds

"Now, young lady, I suppose you're going to tell me you *lost* your driver's license?"

The policeman's tone was skeptical and his gray eyes were dubious as they met Nancy's. The man was a stranger to her, which was unusual, since Nancy knew most of the local police and all were her friends.

"Oh, dear, this is certainly a picklement," wailed Bess. "Now we can't catch that awful Mrs. Channing."

George leaned out of the car. "Officer, this is Nancy Drew," she said. "We're—we're after a thief. Please let us go."

The policeman stared. "You're what? Listen, miss, if that's the case, there are two reasons for my taking you to headquarters. Suppose you tell the chief your story."

17

He directed Nancy to follow him, saying she was "to pull no shenanigans."

Chief of Police McGinnis was surprised to see Nancy. He listened while she explained her predicament of being without a license.

"I just can't figure out what happened to it," she continued. "I know I had it in my wallet yesterday. This morning I forgot to see if it was there."

"I know you have a driver's license, Nancy," the chief assured her. "That's why I'm going to be lenient in your case. You've helped the police department on so many occasions that it's almost as if you were a member of the force."

At this remark the policeman's jaw dropped.

"Oh, thank you, Chief McGinnis," said Nancy gratefully. "I'll make application for a duplicate license at once."

"Good." The officer nodded. "But remember, young lady, keep your car in storage until that new license arrives."

"Chief, *I* have a driver's license," Bess interrupted. "See—it's right here in my pocketbook. I can drive Nancy's car for her."

"You girls!" Chief McGinnis laughed. "You don't miss a trick, do you? Yes, Miss Marvin, I suppose you can act as chauffeur. And now what's this about a thief? Are you up to something we police don't know about?"

Nancy's eyes were teasing as she answered, "I'll let you know the instant I need help!"

"Whew, that was close!" exclaimed George, as the three chums left the police station and hurried back to the car. "I thought you were going to have to tell him about Mrs. Channing and I knew you didn't want to yet."

"No, not until I have some proof she's not honest." There was a thoughtful frown between Nancy's brows. "I wish I could figure out what happened to my license."

"You don't suppose someone stole it, do you?" Bess asked as she slid in behind the steering wheel.

"I can't decide," Nancy admitted. "In the first place, that license isn't worth anything to anybody but me. So *why* would it attract a thief? And *why* would he want my other identification cards?"

"Maybe the thief was looking for money and took the other things by mistake," suggested George. "Did you have much money in your wallet?"

"No, just an emergency five dollars," said Nancy. "I have another purse that I carry silver and bills in. That wasn't tampered with."

"Well, we can put our heads together at luncheon," said Bess. "You're both invited to my house. And, girls, I promise chicken pie and angel cake."

Luncheon was delicious, but what interested

Nancy even more was a message for her from Bess's father. Hearing of the case, Mr. Marvin had telephoned his broker in New York and learned that no such organization as the Forest Fur Company was listed among legitimate stock companies.

"Poor Hannah Gruen!" thought Nancy, deciding to redouble her efforts to find Mrs. Channing.

That afternoon Nancy, Bess, and George stopped at Dr. Britt's office and picked up the list Nurse Compton had prepared. It contained a number of new names of patients who had bought furs or stock from the mysterious Mrs. Channing.

"Where do we call first?" Bess inquired.

"I think Mrs. Clifton Packer would be a good one," decided Nancy. "She's a wealthy widow and bought several hundred shares of stock in the Forest Fur Company."

"Then, Mrs. Packer, here we come," George said with a grin. "Step on it, chauffeur," she commanded, tapping her cousin Bess on the shoulder. "But, for goodness sake—*watch out for traffic cops!*"

The Packer house was a large stone one that looked more like a French chateau than an American residence. A maid, clad in a black uniform and a starched cap and apron, answered the doorbell. She ushered the three girls into the entrance hall.

Mrs. Packer was a stout, talkative woman. She

knew Nancy chiefly by reputation and was plainly curious as to the purpose of the young detective's call.

"Don't tell me I have a mystery here at Oak Manor, Nancy?" she began as soon as the three girls were seated in her luxurious living room.

"Perhaps you have, Mrs. Packer." Nancy smiled. She hastily sketched her reasons for suspecting Mrs. R. I. Channing and her questionable sales activity.

"Why, I'm astounded . . . *simply astounded!*" gasped the plump widow. "Mrs. Channing appeared *so* charming. Such a lady."

"I understand she sold you some furs?" prompted Nancy.

"Oh, she did. She did indeed," babbled Mrs. Packer. "And then, of course, there is that block of stock I bought. I paid her a thousand dollars for that."

Bess and George exchanged startled glances.

"Did Mrs. Channing give you any information about this fur company?" Nancy asked. "Where it's located, for instance?"

"I don't think so," admitted Mrs. Packer. "I just remember her saying they have mink ranches throughout the United States and Canada. That's why I thought the stock was all right. Good mink, you know, is very scarce. And *very* expensive."

"But suppose the stock you bought is worth·

less," said Nancy, and told what Mr. Marvin had learned.

"Oh, dear, I suppose I was foolish," confessed Mrs. Packer. "But it was the lovely mink furs Mrs. Channing showed me that convinced me. You see, I'm quite an authority on peltries."

"Come up to my bedroom, girls," the widow invited, leading the way. "I'll show you what I bought. All mink, you know, isn't equally fine. There are four different grades. The best fur comes from the northern United States and Canada. It's the cold weather that makes it lustrous and triply thick."

Mrs. Packer opened a closet and removed a luxurious mink cape. "The minute Mrs. Channing showed this to me I knew I *had* to have it," she rattled on. "Notice the rich dark-brown color —how alive and silky the fur is!

"That shows the cape was made from young mink. In older animals, the fur is much coarser and the pelts are larger, too. A sure indication that you have a less valuable piece of merchandise."

George winked at Nancy. They were surely getting Mrs. Channing's sales talk secondhand!

Bess giggled. "Young mink, old mink—who cares?" she said. "I'd settle for any kind of a mink coat."

They went back to the living room. Mrs.

Packer rang a bell and ordered her maid, Hilda, to serve tea. After the maid had left, their hostess dimpled coyly.

"I just love tea parties—don't you?" Evidently she was not too concerned about her missing thousand dollars. "Hilda makes the most divine little cakes. I served them when I had the party for Mrs. Channing."

"What!" George burst out, then added apologetically, "I'm sorry."

Mrs. Packer exclaimed that she had held a party for Mrs. Channing to introduce certain friends who were always "looking for bargains in clothes." The friends had purchased both furs and stock. Nancy was about to ask their names when the woman abruptly changed the subject.

"Now that you're here, Nancy Drew, I want to consult you about the disappearance of my favorite earrings."

Nancy looked doubtful. "I don't know, Mrs. Packer. I'm pretty busy just now," she began. "Perhaps you just misplaced them?"

"Of course I didn't," her hostess protested. "I always put everything back in my jewel case the minute I take it off. Besides, I was very careful of those earrings. They're part of a valuable set.

"See, I'm wearing the brooch to it. Nancy, how would it be if you take it with you, so you can trace the earrings for me?" the widow continued, removing the pin and extending it to the girl.

Despite the fact that Nancy had one mystery to solve and was to help her father on another, she found herself saying, just as Hilda walked in with the tea tray:

"I'll do what I can, Mrs. Packer. When did you first miss your jewelry?"

As the woman pondered the question, Nancy saw Hilda stop short. The maid placed the tray on top of the piano and hastened back to the kitchen, as if she had forgotten something. Perhaps the napkins, Nancy thought, but she immediately noticed them protruding over the corner of the tray. Did Hilda's action have anything to do with the conversation?

"Do you remember when you missed your jewelry?" Nancy prompted Mrs. Packer, who seemingly had not noticed the strange procedure.

"Oh, yes, now I remember," the woman said, her hands fluttering in agitation. "It was the day after that party."

George shot a glance toward Nancy, but let the young detective do the talking.

"Do you know of anybody at the party who might have wanted the earrings?" Nancy asked.

Hilda hastened back from the kitchen, picked up the tray, and approached her mistress. She appeared pale and nervous.

"No, unless it was— Why, Nancy, do you

think it could have been Mrs. Channing, the woman you said sold me the fake fur stock?''

At Mrs. Packer's words an agonized wail burst from Hilda. She went chalk white.

"O-oh!" she cried.

Nancy looked up just in time to see the tray tilt precariously in the maid's hands. Hilda clutched at the dishes, but too late. The tray slipped from her grasp!

The top of the teapot fell off and a cascade of hot water poured down upon the arm of Hilda's startled mistress. And with it the cups and saucers clattered to the sofa.

Hilda waited no longer. With a terrified scream she turned on her heel and went running from the room.

CHAPTER IV

More Trouble

"Oh! I'm burned!" Mrs. Packer cried out. She jumped up and shook her wet sleeve. "Such stupid clumsiness!" she sputtered, seizing a napkin and swabbing her arm.

"Nancy," she went on, "did you notice how Hilda jumped when I spoke of my stolen earrings? It's plain the girl knows something. Why, she may even have taken them herself!"

"She certainly acted strangely," agreed George.

"Yes—and while we've been talking, she's escaped!" Bess added excitedly.

"Hilda looks like an honest person," said Nancy in defense. "I think she's only worried or scared. Mrs. Packer, do you mind if I look for your maid?"

"Go right ahead," the widow replied. "But I think I should call the police."

"Wait a little, please," Nancy urged. "And tell

me, are there any other servants in the house?"

"No," said Mrs. Packer. "My butler and cook took the afternoon off. If Hilda hasn't run away already, she's probably in her room. That's on the third floor. The second door to the left."

Nancy found Hilda's bedroom door tightly closed. But she knew by the sound of hysterical sobbing that the maid was inside. She knocked softly.

"Hilda, let me in," she called. "Don't be afraid. I just want to help you."

"Go 'way," said a muffled voice. "Mrs. Packer— she wants to send me to prison."

"No. I want to talk to you, Hilda," pleaded the young detective. "I'm your friend. Won't you listen to me, please?"

The sympathy in Nancy's voice must have convinced the nervous woman, for she opened the door. "I was packing my suitcase," she admitted, stabbing at her reddened eyes with a handkerchief. "Oh, Miss Drew, I've been such a fool!"

"We're all foolish now and then," soothed Nancy, as she led the maid gently to the bed and sat down beside her. "Now, Hilda, why don't you tell me about it?" she suggested.

Ten minutes later Nancy and a subdued but calmer Hilda rejoined the others in the living room. Nancy's blue eyes twinkled as she addressed her hostess.

"Mrs. Packer, Hilda hasn't committed any crime. Her only mistake was that *she did exactly as you did!*"

"What do you mean?"

"Simply this," explained Nancy. "Hilda heard Mrs. Channing talk about the stock in the Forest Fur Company and how it would make her a lot of money. When she saw you buy some of it, Hilda decided to do the same thing."

"Ya," said Hilda, bobbing her white-blond head. "That's just what I did. I think what's good for a smart lady like Mrs. Packer is good for me."

Mrs. Packer's grim face softened. "Why, Hilda," she said. "In a way, that's a compliment."

"Of course it is," said Nancy. "Hilda feels doubly bad because the money she used was the twenty-five dollars she borrowed on her salary to send to her family in Europe."

"Never mind," said her mistress hastily. "I'll see that you don't lose by this, Hilda. Suppose you get busy now and clear away those broken cups and saucers."

Nancy and her friends left, the valuable brooch pinned on the young detective's blouse. She promised to try finding the earrings as soon as possible.

"I'm glad poor Hilda didn't lose her money and her job," said Bess, as the three girls headed for

Nancy's house. "I think Mrs. Packer was to blame, anyway."

"But we didn't get much further in tracking down Mrs. Channing," George remarked.

"No," said Nancy. "But I believe we've advanced a bit. We'd nearly forgotten *Mr*. Channing. I'm sure that he's a part of our crossword puzzle."

"And what a puzzle!" Bess sighed as she drove into the Drew garage. She and George walked home.

Togo, Nancy's alert little terrier, was waiting for her when Nancy stepped into the house. The little fellow scampered joyfully ahead of her as she climbed the stairs and went into her father's deserted study. Togo cocked his head. He was hoping his mistress was going to play a game with him.

"I love this room, Togo," Nancy confided. "It makes me feel so close to Dad. Let's pretend he's here, shall we?" She sat down in the big leather chair and held out her arms to the eager dog.

"You sit right here . . . on my lap . . . Togo. That's it. Now we'll hold our conference.

"First of all, I know what Dad would advise. He'd say: 'Use your head, daughter! You can't just chase after this Mrs. Channing as if she were a butterfly. You must outsmart her!'

"Hmm-m, that's right," mused the girl. "Probably Mrs. Channing has exhausted her prospects in River Heights. This means she has moved into new territory. But where?

"Got any suggestions, Togo? Speak up, boy!"

At the word "speak" the little terrier gave a sharp bark. "Oh, I see." Nancy grinned. "You advise that we try one town in each direction from here. If Mrs. Channing has been seen in any of these places, we'll know whether she has headed north, south, east, or west. And a very good idea it is."

Nancy heaved a sigh of relief and set Togo on the floor. "Okay. Conference is over," she announced. "Now we'll go and see about dinner, partner."

Nancy spent the evening at the telephone. First, she followed up the rest of the names on Miss Compton's list. No information of value came of this.

Next, she called several out-of-town physicians who were friends of Dr. Britt's. To her satisfaction she found that three had been visited by Mr. and Mrs. Channing. Later the physicians called her back to say certain patients of theirs had been approached by the couple and some had bought furs and stock.

When Bess and George arrived the next morning, Nancy greeted them with, "We're going to Masonville. Why? Because it's north of here."

"Hypers! Nancy, it's too early in the day for riddles," George complained.

Nancy smiled mysteriously, then said all of Mrs.
Channing's victims to the west, south, and east of
River Heights had been called upon at least a
month before.

"So our saleswoman won't go back there,"
Nancy theorized. "But apparently she hasn't
tackled Masonville yet. If we can only find her
at work there—"

"Let's go! George said impatiently.

Part way along the road to Masonville, Bess suddenly gasped. "Our gas gauge says *empty*. I hope
we don't get stuck."

Luck favored the girls. A quarter of a mile
farther on they came to a gas station. The proprietor was a gaunt, gray-haired man in frayed
overalls. Nancy lowered a window of the convertible and asked him to fill the tank. Then she
said:

"Has a middle-aged woman in a mink coat and
driving a long, black car stopped here lately?"

The old fellow looked at her shrewdly and
scratched one ear. "Was the lady purty and was
that a fine mink coat?" he countered.

At his words Nancy's heart gave an exultant
leap. "Oh, you've seen her, then! Do you mind
telling us when it was?"

"No, I don't mind," said the man. "The lady
come by here yesterday mornin' on her way to
Masonville. My wife was with me. The minute

she spotted that coat she began oh-in' and ah-in', the way women folks do."

"Did she sell your wife a fur piece?" Bess interrupted, unable to restrain her excitement.

The man shook his head. "Nope. She didn't sell us nothin', young lady. But she claimed to be from a big fur outfit. Even offered to get my wife a mink coat cheap—that is, if we'd buy some stock in her company first."

"Did she show you this stock?" persisted Nancy.

"She did, but I'm an old Vermonter myself. I never heard o' that town, Dunstan Lake, listed on the certificate."

"Did you ask her about it?"

"Sure, miss. She said Dunstan Lake was only a village with too few people for a post office. Sounded fishy to me."

"How right you are!" George said grimly. "I'm glad you didn't buy anything from her."

As the girls drove off, Bess cried enthusiastically, "We're on the right track!"

Masonville was only five miles from the gas station. The cousins were excited as they drove into town, convinced that they were on Mrs. Channing's trail at last.

"Let's not celebrate too soon," Nancy cautioned. "Mrs. Channing may have finished her work here too and driven farther north. But we'll investigate."

"I'll park in front of this bank," said Bess.

"All right," Nancy agreed. "We can walk from here. But first let's decide what to do."

"Shouldn't we try the hotels, Nancy?" George suggested. "If Mrs. Channing is registered at one of them, it might save us the trouble of going to any other place."

"Do you know the names of any hotels here?" Bess asked.

Nancy thought a moment. "There's the Mansion House, but I don't think Mrs. Channing would like that. It's a commercial hotel."

"Isn't the Palace in Masonville?" George recalled. "Famous for lobster or something?"

"Yes, but it's no longer a hotel, Dad told me. It's an office building now."

"We're getting nowhere fast," George groaned. "Let's go ask a police—"

She broke off abruptly as Bess's eyes suddenly grew wide with fear and she whispered excitedly:

"Girls! Look at those two men across the street! They're staring at us as if we'd just escaped from jail."

"You're being silly," George remarked, not taking her scary cousin seriously.

"I mean it," Bess insisted. "You look yourself."

George turned to look and Nancy leaned forward to observe the men. One was a short, stout man in a gray overcoat and soft gray hat. The other was slim and younger. He wore a blue mackinaw with the collar turned up, and a cap pulled low on his forehead.

At a nod from him, the stout man walked determinedly across the street toward the convertible, with the younger man close behind.

As the girls watched, the two men slowly circled the car and examined the license plate at its rear. Then a big hand pulled open the door beside Bess.

"Which of you is Nancy Drew?" he demanded in a deep voice.

"I am," Nancy admitted. "Why do you want to know?"

"*You!*" said the stout man. "You're wanted for shoplifting, Nancy Drew. And, here and now, I place you under arrest!"

CHAPTER V

The Second Nancy

THE MAN in the gray overcoat motioned for the three girls to get out of the car. For several seconds they sat still, too astonished to say a word. Nancy faced the men and said calmly:

"Suppose you tell me who you are, and why you're making this ridiculous charge."

The stout man opened his coat. A police badge gleamed on his vest pocket. His companion showed one also.

"We're plain-clothes men," he explained. "We were told to pick up a car with this license number and a Nancy Drew who owns it. Now don't try to get away. Just come along to headquarters peacefully."

"Y-you can't arrest Nancy," Bess said tremulously. "Why, she's the most honest girl in the world."

"Besides," George spoke up indignantly, "she's a detective. You'd better be careful what you say."

"Ho, so she claims to be a detective, does she?" the stout man snorted. "I suppose she was a detective when she entered a fur store here and stole two expensive mink scarfs?"

"What!" George cried. "That's absurd."

"I did no such thing," Nancy protested.

"Oh, yes, you did," insisted the slim fellow. "After you showed your license and charged a cheap fur piece, you took two expensive furs that you *didn't* charge! What did you do with them?"

Nancy's mind was working fast. The woman who had her driver's license was pretending to be Nancy Drew! If it were Mrs. Channing, she probably had altered the age and other statistics on the card. Nancy decided to go to the police station at once and exonerate herself.

"Come on, girls," she said, climbing into the car.

The men squeezed in, and the stout detective pointed out the way to the Masonville police headquarters. There a Sergeant Wilks took down Nancy's name and address.

"You live in River Heights and your name is Drew?" he inquired. "Any relation to Mr. Drew, the lawyer?"

"My father," said Nancy.

"Good grief!" gulped the sergeant. You never

can tell *where* these juvenile delinquents will come from nowadays."

Nancy turned scarlet and protested. George sputtered. Bess seemingly had disappeared.

"Silence!" the officer ordered.

As he repeated the charge against Nancy, the outer door was suddenly flung open. A distinguished-looking man burst in, followed by Bess.

"Judge Hartgrave!" Nancy cried, rushing forward to greet her father's old friend. "You're just the person I need!"

"So your friend Bess told me." Nancy threw Bess a grateful look.

"You—you know the judge?" the sergeant stammered.

"Very well. He helped me solve a mystery once."

Judge Hartgrave turned to the officer. "This is outrageous, Sergeant! Why are you holding my friend Nancy Drew?"

The officer reddened at the rebuke. He explained about the thief who had stolen the mink scarfs from the Masonville Fur Company, and how the woman had identified herself as Nancy Drew and shown a driver's license to prove it.

"I can't understand it," said the judge, shaking his head.

"It's because my driver's license was stolen two days ago, Judge," said Nancy. "I've been telling these officers someone evidently is using it, but they won't believe me."

"I see." Judge Hartgrave frowned. "Let's call in that fur shop owner and settle this matter properly."

The man was summoned to headquarters. He looked at Nancy and shook his head. "She's not the same person," he said positively. "The thief was older."

"Was the woman wearing a mink coat and were her eyes blue and her hair blue-black?" Nancy inquired.

"Why—uh—yes," agreed the man. "She was a striking brunette."

The three girls exchanged knowing glances. Mrs. Channing, no doubt of that!

"Well, Nancy, that settles it," said Judge Hartgrave. "I'm sure you're free to go now. Isn't that right, Sergeant?"

"Sure, she can leave," grumbled the discomfited Wilks. "Only I'd like to ask Miss Drew a question first."

Nancy and her two friends had already started for the door but she turned and paused. "Yes, Sergeant?"

"This dark-haired woman you were asking about. Can you tell us where to find her?"

"I wish I could," said Nancy. "I only know that sometimes she calls herself Mrs. Channing. Besides being a shoplifter, she sells fake stock."

"Um, sounds like an all-around bad egg," nodded Wilks. "But the Masonville police force is on its toes. We'll get her!"

The girls walked with Judge Hartgrave to his office next door, and Nancy thanked him for his help. He asked for more details concerning the mystery. After he had heard them, the judge remarked:

"I've spent many summers in Vermont, but I've never heard of Dunstan Lake." He turned to his telephone. "It won't take long to find out where it is."

A moment later he was talking to a friend at the Vermont State House in Montpelier. When the judge finished his conversation, he reported to Nancy that there was no such place as Dunstan Lake anywhere in the state of Vermont.

"You have a real mystery on your hands, young lady," he said. "Let me know if I can help you."

"I surely will," Nancy promised.

As the girls walked back to the car, Bess said something was puzzling her. If Mrs. Channing had Nancy's license, when and how had she taken it?

"It must have been when Mrs. Martin and I left her alone on the living-room sofa after the accident," Nancy replied. "When Mrs. Channing regained consciousness, she must have slipped the papers out of my wallet. It was in my coat on a chair."

"Shoplifters *are* quick with their hands," Bess nodded.

"Yes, they're much like pickpockets," Nancy agreed. "Well, here's my car, girls. It's time we headed farther north."

"North?" chorused the cousins. Aren't we going to look for Mrs. Channing in Masonville?"

"After that theft, I'm sure she left town as quickly as possible," Nancy answered. "Since she wouldn't dare turn back, I believe she continued north."

For the next hour Nancy's little convertible traveled down the highway as fast as Bess could drive it and still keep within the speed limit. Here and there the girls stopped at small towns and inquired if anyone had seen a woman of Mrs. Channing's description in a long, black car.

At last, tired and discouraged, they reached the town of Winchester and stopped in front of the Crestview Hotel. George went inside to make the usual inquiry and soon came rushing back.

"Oh, girls, *we've found her!*" she cried excitedly. "The desk clerk said a dark-haired woman in a mink coat had registered at the hotel the night before. She isn't in now."

"Where did she go?" Bess demanded. "I'll bet to rob somebody."

"Probably," George replied. "But listen to this: I saw the hotel register. And, Nancy, she's still pretending to be you. The name Nancy Drew is written down as bold as you please."

Nancy's eyes flashed angrily. "I've always been proud of my name and I certainly resent having it connected with a thief! Come on, girls! Mrs. Channing can't get away with this! We'll stand guard until she comes back."

The lobby of the Crestview was warm and spacious. Nancy suggested that they wait in the shadow of the newsstand so Mrs. Channing would not see the girls and make a hasty exit before she could be caught.

The trap seemed perfect. But when, after an hour of tedious waiting, their quarry failed to arrive, Nancy became impatient. She walked up to the desk.

"We're here to see a guest registered as Nancy Drew," she told the clerk. "Possibly she came in by another entrance?"

"That's impossible," the man said. "There's no other entrance except a back door used by our employees. However, I'll call Room 202 on the house phone if you like."

There was no answer from the room. Nancy decided to take the clerk, Mr. Evans, into her confidence. When he heard the story, the man became worried and offered to unlock the suspect's room to see if there were any evidence to prove Nancy's theory.

When they reached the room, Bess and George stayed in the hall to watch for Mrs. Channing. Nancy followed Mr. Evans inside. He glanced about, opened the closet door, and gave a cry of dismay.

"Her bags are gone! She's left without paying her bill!"

The fake fur saleswoman had been there, all right. Nancy could detect the scent of her exotic perfume in the air, and traces of powder lay on the dressing table.

Nancy walked quickly to a window, lifted it, and stared down at the ground ten feet below. There she could see scrambled footprints and several deep indentations in the snow.

Mr. Evans also popped his head out to take a look. "See anything?" he asked.

"I think I can figure out how Mrs. Channing got away," said the young detective. "She slipped up here by the servants' stairway and dropped her bags out the window. Then she went down the stairs again, picked up her luggage, and hurried off."

"The cheat! I'll make her pay! She can't get away with this!" Mr. Evans sputtered.

"You'll have to catch her first," Nancy thought. Aloud she said, "Perhaps Mrs. Channing left something behind that will give us a clue to where she's going."

As she spoke, Nancy was moving slowly about the room, her eyes searching the floor and furniture. Methodically she opened and shut bureau drawers. Empty, all of them! The wastebasket contained several lipstick-stained tissues. Apparently Mrs. Channing had taken time to make herself look attractive!

Suddenly Nancy gave a cry of triumph and stooped to pick up something from beneath the bed. In her hands she held a small black label used by stores to identify their merchandise.

Printed on it in gold letters was the telltale inscription: *Masonville Fur Company.*

CHAPTER VI

Locked In

"WHAT'S wrong, Mr. Evans?" asked an excited voice from the doorway.

The speaker was a plump woman of faded beauty who peered curiously into the room. At her question the hotel clerk whirled nervously.

"Why—uh—good morning, Mrs. Plimpton. We're merely looking for a guest who occupied this room," he answered.

"Miss Drew, you mean," said Mrs. Plimpton. "I haven't seen her since breakfast. We ate together and had a nice chat."

Hearing the word "chat" Nancy suspected another stock sale. "I came a long way to see this lady," she said. "I wonder if I might talk to you privately, Mrs. Plimpton?"

"Why, certainly," she agreed. "My room's just across the hall. We can talk there."

While George and Bess waited for her in the hotel lobby, Nancy listened to the woman's story of becoming acquainted with "Miss Drew." Mrs. Plimpton proved to be a friendly, unsuspecting person and Nancy had no difficulty in finding out what she wanted to know about the crafty Mrs. Channing. During breakfast Mrs. Plimpton had admired the fur coat which the younger woman wore.

"If you like mink, I can sell you a fur scarf at half price," Mrs. Channing had suggested. "To be frank, I'm a little hard pressed for money just now."

A little later, in Mrs. Plimpton's room, Mrs. Channing had followed her usual tricky methods. She had persuaded the other woman to buy the fur scarf and also to invest five hundred dollars in stock. When Nancy told Mrs. Plimpton that the value of the stock was questionable, tears came to the woman's eyes.

"If I've made a poor bargain and wasted our family savings, my husband will never forgive me," she confided. "It was just that this woman seemed so kind and sincere."

"I'm terribly sorry about the whole thing," said Nancy. "Mrs. Plimpton, in your conversation with her, did 'Miss Drew' give you any hint as to where she might be going from here?"

The woman thought a moment, then shook her

head. "She talked as if she planned to stay here for some time."

Nancy came to the conclusion that Mrs. Channing must have caught a glimpse of her as the girls entered the hotel. For the moment, the woman seemed to have outsmarted the detective again. Then suddenly Nancy thought of the Masonville fur store.

"May I see the scarf you bought?" she asked.

"Certainly," Mrs. Plimpton replied, going to the wardrobe.

The fur piece was indeed beautiful, but there was no label on it. No doubt the one Nancy had found had once been sewed to the lining.

"May I please use your phone?" she requested.

Nancy called the Masonville Fur Company and learned from the proprietor that every fur piece of theirs had MFC stamped on one of the skins. At the time of purchase the date was added. The young detective thanked him and hung up.

Borrowing some scissors, she quickly opened the lining of the scarf. Near the neckline there was a telltale MFC but no date mark! Nancy explained her find to Mrs. Plimpton and what it meant.

"I'll let that fur company know," the woman said tearfully. "Oh, dear, what will my husband say?"

Nancy leaned down and patted her hand.

"Don't give up hope, Mrs. Plimpton," she encouraged. "We'll try to get your money back for you. I'm sure we'll catch that thief. By the way, her name is not Drew—it's Channing. If you should ever see her, be sure to call the police."

After promising to do all she could for Mrs. Plimpton, Nancy went down to the lobby.

"Well, it's about time you appeared!" George complained.

"Nancy Drew, don't you think we *ever* have to eat?" Bess asked. "I've had nothing but a hamburger since breakfast. I'm practically grown together in the middle!"

"Then prepare to gorge yourself, my pet." Nancy grinned. "I saw a nice little tearoom, called the Golden Swan, only a few blocks from here. We'll go there at once."

On the way to the tearoom, Nancy brought her friends up to date on the mystery. "And, girls, hold on to your hats!" she warned. "That fur piece Mrs. Plimpton purchased bears the Masonville Fur Company's mark."

George whistled. "Hypers! That's what I call piling up evidence," she praised. "If we ever do find Mrs. Channing, she'll sure have a lot of counts against her."

Bess asked Nancy if she thought stealing furs and selling them was what the woman had been doing all along.

"I'm not sure where she got her first supply," said Nancy. "But evidently business has been so good that she ran out of merchandise and had to resort to shoplifting."

"Mr. Evans reported her to the Winchester police for not paying her room bill," George remarked. "That was a foolish thing for her to do."

"Yes, it was. But I don't believe Mrs. Channing intended to cheat the hotel," said Nancy. "I think something frightened her away—probably my arrival."

As they entered the Golden Swan, Bess said, "Let's stop playing cops and robbers for a bit. I want to concentrate on food!"

The hostess led the girls to a small table beside the window. Here, for the next twenty minutes, they were content to relax and enjoy the delicious food.

"Where do you want to drive next?" Bess asked when they had finished.

"I have another idea," Nancy replied. "Before we leave here, I thought we should canvass all the exclusive shops in town. Find out if they've missed any furs. You girls know—"

Nancy's voice trailed away. She was staring through the window and down the street. An instant before she had seen a slender, elegantly dressed woman walking briskly along the opposite side of the street.

Her hair was shiny blue-black! Mrs. Channing! Nancy rose hastily from the table. "Wait for me," she said quickly to Bess and George, and dashed from the tearoom.

Nancy hurried across the street and followed the woman. Mrs. Channing was moving along so rapidly that the girl had no chance to be subtle in her shadowing. To keep her eye on her target she had to weave agilely among other pedestrians.

Mrs. Channing paused to look in a gift-shop window. Nancy nearly caught up to her. But the thief had used the plate glass as a mirror!

A swift turn on her heels, and she was running down the street. A moment later she slipped into a small fur shop.

Nancy looked up and down the street for a policeman. None was in sight.

"I'll have to handle this alone!" she thought and increased her speed.

Reaching the fur shop, Nancy gazed cautiously through the plate-glass window. The place was artistically lighted and tastefully furnished. She noted the deep-piled rug and the ivory and gold showcase. Several choice silver fox and mink fur pieces lay in it. But Mrs. Channing was not in sight.

Nancy opened the door and stepped inside. A small, round man moved briskly to meet her, followed by a small and equally round woman.

"Something my wife and I can do for you, miss?" the man asked.

"I came to inquire about a woman I saw enter this place a minute ago," Nancy replied. "A tall brunette in a mink coat."

"Brunette? Mink coat?"

The storekeeper raised his eyebrows and shook his head, at the same time glancing quickly at his wife. "Perhaps you are mistaken?"

"But she must have come in here. I saw her myself," Nancy persisted. "It's important that I find her."

"And who are you, please?" the man demanded.

"My name is Nancy Drew and—"

Nancy got no further. With a yelp of rage the little man leaped toward her and pinned the girl's hands behind her back. At the same time his wife threw a dark cloth over their captive's head.

Nancy struggled, but the determined couple overpowered her. With a victorious cry they dragged her to a rear room.

"Unlock that closet quick!" the man ordered.

Nancy heard the click of a door latch. Then she was shoved among some fur coats hanging in the closet. The door slammed shut, and a key turned in the lock.

"You can't come in here and rob us!" the proprietor yelled excitedly. *"We know you for a thief!"*

CHAPTER VII

Curious Payment

THE CLOSET in which Nancy was a prisoner was not only dark but stuffy. Fur garments pressed against her in the crowded quarters, nearly suffocating her.

From the shop, Nancy could hear the murmur of excited voices. She pressed an ear anxiously to a crack in the door and listened.

"I say we call the police at once!" the woman shrilled. "Tell them we captured this thief ourselves and no thanks to their protection."

"But, Mama, suppose the lady in the fur coat was mistaken?" persisted the proprietor. "All we know is that she rushed in here and warned us a thief named Nancy Drew was coming to steal furs."

"Well, *I* believe the lady," insisted his wife. "This girl admitted she was Nancy Drew, didn't she? That's proof enough for me."

51

Nancy's heart sank. "Oh, dear, how silly can people get?" she groaned. "How Mrs. Channing must be laughing at the trick she played on me!"

Suddenly Nancy heard the shop door open. Her first inclination was to cry out for help. But she decided to wait a moment to be sure this was not another enemy.

"Pardon me," said a voice. "Did a blond girl in a red coat come in here?"

George! Bless her, thought Nancy!

"Why do you ask?" the proprietor demanded suspiciously.

"Because she's a friend of ours," piped Bess's voice. "She left us in a tearoom a few minutes ago. We saw her enter this shop."

A moment of silence was broken by the woman's voice. "What was her name?"

"Nancy Drew."

"She's a thief and you've come to help her steal!" the woman shrieked excitedly. "Papa, let's lock them up too!"

"What!" George blurted.

Nancy waited no longer. Doubling up her fists, she banged on the closed door with all her might. *"Bess! George!* I'm locked in here!" she shouted.

There was a startled exclamation, then the sound of running feet. In a second the key turned in the lock and the closet door swung open.

"Nancy! What happened?" Bess gasped.

"Mrs. Channing told these people to hold me," explained Nancy breathlessly. "She said I was a thief."

The man frowned. "Who is Mrs. Channing, please?"

"The woman in the fur coat," said Nancy. "She stole two mink scarfs in Masonville yesterday. I believe she planned to rob you but saw me coming."

"Nancy's a detective," Bess spoke up.

The mouths of the shop owners dropped open. "A detective?" they chorused, and the man added quickly, "I meant no harm, miss."

Nancy was amused at the change in their manner, but she had no time for recriminations.

"Where did Mrs. Channing go?" she asked.

"Out the back door," the chagrined proprietor pointed. "I'm sorry we treated you so badly, young lady."

"Never mind. Come on, girls!" Nancy called, dashing out the rear door. "Maybe we can pick up that woman's trail."

But picking up the trail of the quick-witted Mrs. Channing proved to be as difficult as before. She was not hiding in any of the alleys or shops in the vicinity. Although the girls cruised slowly up and down the streets of Winchester for a long time, and inquired at two other hotels and all the fur shops, no one could give them any information about Mrs. Channing.

"The woman vanishes in smoke like an evil genie," sighed Bess.

George grinned. "Maybe that's why we didn't find her. We've searched everything but the town's smokestacks!"

"Nancy," said Bess, "it will be dark in a few hours. Why don't we go home? Besides, I have a date tonight to go skating."

"Speaking of sports, there's to be a bobsled party on North Hill tomorrow night," George interjected. "Jack Daly called me. And if you'd like to, come along, Nancy."

The young detective smiled. "Ned offered to come down from college for it. But I may have to leave for Montreal any minute."

Surprisingly enough, it was on the girls' way back to River Heights that they picked up another clue to Mrs. Channing's whereabouts. At a service station an employee informed them that a long, black car with a crooked bumper and dented fenders had stopped there for gas.

"Yes," the attendant admitted, "the driver was a dark woman in a fur coat. I remember her especially, for she seemed terribly nervous—kept looking back over her shoulder all the time." At the woman's order he had filled up the gas tank, because she said she was going on quite a long trip.

"Did she tell you where?" Nancy asked.

"No, she didn't, but it might have been Vermont."

"Vermont!" the three girls cried out together.

The startled attendant asked what was so strange about that. Before Nancy could stop Bess, she had told most of the story about Mrs. Channing. The man was interested at once.

"You know that woman had two extra fur coats on the back seat," he said. "The car had a Vermont license, so that's why I said she might be headed there."

Nancy was excited over the information.

"Thank you," she said. "You've been of real help." She paid the bill and they started off.

"I suppose our next stop is Vermont?" Bess teased.

"By telephone," Nancy answered, and put in two long-distance calls to Vermont.

The Bureau of Motor Vehicles informed Nancy that a driver's license had been issued to a Mitzi Channing. A call to the address which Mitzi had given when she had applied for the license revealed that she no longer was living there and her present whereabouts was unknown. Nancy next called the local police and asked them to alert the Vermont authorities.

When she reached home, Hannah Gruen greeted her with a broad smile. Nancy could tell by the satisfied way in which the housekeeper bustled about to make her comfortable that she was pleased about something.

"I'm sorry you had such a long, tedious trip," she said.

"Oh, it wasn't tedious," Nancy assured her. "In fact, I picked up some good clues."

"What were you girls doing, anyway? Trailing that nice Mrs. Channing?" Hannah went on.

"Nice!" Nancy bristled. "I certainly wouldn't call her nice."

"That's because you're prejudiced," said the housekeeper. "You thought that stock I bought from Mrs. Channing was no good. Well—it is!"

"What makes you think so?" Nancy asked.

"Because in the afternoon mail I received some money from the Forest Fur Company—a nice fat dividend," Hannah finished triumphantly.

Nancy stared at her in amazement. "You can't mean that fake fur company actually paid you?" she demanded incredulously.

"They certainly did," said Hannah. "And Mrs. Martin phoned me that she got a payment too."

"Why—why—it simply doesn't make sense," stammered Nancy as she bounced to her feet and hastily made for the telephone. "I'm going to call Mrs. Clifton Packer."

The wealthy widow greeted Nancy cordially. She admitted having received a sizable dividend in the mail. But, unlike the other two women, Mrs. Packer was not too enthusiastic about it.

"I suppose the payment was not very large," Nancy remarked, thinking that the wealthy widow was used to receiving far more sizable dividends from other stocks.

"Oh, no, it's not that," Mrs. Packer replied. "Nancy, there's something *queer* about the way the money was sent," she said sharply. "I think you should investigate at once!"

CHAPTER VIII

Clue in New York

NANCY's fingers tightened on the telephone receiver. "You say the dividend payment looks queer, Mrs. Packer?" she prompted.

"Yes. As you might guess, I have a lot of stock in various companies," the woman replied. "They always send their dividends by check. Checks signed by their treasurer."

"And the payment from Forest Fur Company was different?"

"It certainly was," said the widow. "It was merely a money order mailed from New York. I'm sure no legitimate business would work that way."

"Thank you, Mrs. Packer. That's just what I wanted to know," said Nancy gratefully.

"Well, what did she say?" inquired Hannah Gruen, as Nancy put down the telephone.

"Mrs. Packer agrees with me that something is

wrong," said Nancy. "Do you still have the letter that came with your dividend?"

"There wasn't any letter." The housekeeper frowned. "Just the money order in an envelope."

"Then may I see the envelope, please?" Nancy persisted.

Mrs. Gruen had cashed the money order. Unfortunately she could not remember how she had disposed of the envelope. It was only after ten minutes of fuss and flurry that the envelope was finally located in a trash can.

Nancy smoothed out the crumpled bit of paper and studied the sender's address in the upper left-hand corner. There was no name; only a smudged address in New York City.

"Who sent those money orders?" she asked herself. "It couldn't have been Mrs. Channing. She was in River Heights at the very time this envelope was mailed."

Clearly, then, Nancy thought, the woman must have a confederate in New York—a criminal partner to whom she sent a list of her victims and who must have mailed the dividends.

Was it Mr. Channing?

Nancy set her chin determinedly. "This is the best clue I have—and I won't lose any time in following it," she decided. "If Dad doesn't need me yet, I'll take the eight o'clock plane for New York tomorrow."

After supper Nancy telephoned Mr. Drew at his Montreal hotel and told him what she had done so far on her case. Then she asked if she might have a little more time for a quick trip to New York before she joined him.

"If you think it's important, go ahead," the lawyer replied. "I've found some extra work up here that'll keep me busy a few days. In the meantime, maybe you'll solve the mystery of Mrs. Channing."

Next morning Nancy took her seat on the big passenger plane with a thrill of pleasure. She always enjoyed trips to New York. The city itself was big and exciting. But even more she loved to visit her Aunt Eloise.

Aunt Lou, as Nancy called her, was her father's younger sister. And more than once the schoolteacher had assisted her niece in solving a mystery.

By noontime Nancy was ringing the bell of her aunt's apartment. Eloise Drew greeted her with a warm hug and an exclamation of delight.

"Nancy, darling! You're the answer to a big wish," cried her aunt. "Here I was with a long week end on my hands and nothing to do. And now, presto! In you pop with that telltale gleam in your eyes. A gleam that says you're involved in another mystery. Right?"

"Right!" Her niece laughed. "And I hope you'll help me."

While she and Aunt Lou prepared a light luncheon, Nancy told her story, ending with the episode about the questionable dividend payment.

"What do you plan to do about it, Nancy?" her aunt inquired.

"Go to the address on that envelope, Aunt Lou. I suspect Mrs. Channing's husband may be there, and if he's the one who sent those money orders, I'll notify the police."

"I'll go with you," the schoolteacher announced.

After she and her niece had finished luncheon they started out. It didn't take long by subway for Nancy and her aunt to reach the run-down district of the address on the envelope. To their amazement it proved to be a hotel. The place was small and shabby. A bored clerk looked up from the novel he was reading as the two approached his desk.

"I'm looking for Mr. R. I. Channing," said Nancy. "Is he registered here?"

"Channing?" mumbled the clerk. "No, we haven't anybody by that name."

Nancy tried hard to conceal her disappointment. "Perhaps I was mistaken in the name," she said quickly. "But you do have a guest who works for the Forest Fur Company?"

"No. Don't think I ever heard of such a firm," the clerk drawled. "Look, young lady, this is a residential hotel. We don't handle business and—"

"Pardon me. Did you mention the Forest Fur Company?" interrupted a voice behind Nancy.

The speaker was an overdressed, red-haired woman in her early forties. As Nancy turned to face her, the stranger gave the young detective a glittering, artificial smile.

"I'm Miss Reynolds," she explained. "I live in this hotel and I couldn't help but hear your question. I believe I know the very person you're looking for. I'm a stockholder in his company," she finished proudly.

Nancy's heart leaped. "At last we're getting somewhere," she thought. Aloud she said, "I'm Nancy Drew and this is my aunt. Would you mind telling me where to find him?"

"Why, Mr. Sidney Boyd occupies the suite next to mine," went on the red-haired woman loftily. "Such a *gentleman*, Mr. Boyd! So considerate and *such a student of the theater!* Why, do you know what he said of my performance in *Wild Lilacs*, Miss Drew? He said—"

"I'm sure it was very complimentary, Miss Reynolds," Nancy cut in hastily, when she foresaw that the woman might ramble on indefinitely. "Do you mind telling me how you happened to purchase Forest Fur Company stock? Did Mr. Boyd sell it to you?"

"Of course he did. But only after I *coaxed* him," admitted the actress, coyly rolling her eyes.

"It isn't every day that a girl can buy into the mink fur business."

The clerk had listened to this conversation wide-eyed. Now he waited until Miss Reynolds nodded a good-bye to the Drews and sauntered slowly toward the elevator.

"Huh! So Bunny Reynolds calls herself an actress, does she!" he snorted. "Why, she hasn't had a theater engagement in years."

"What about your other guest, Mr. Sidney Boyd?" Nancy prompted.

"Yes, what about him?" Aunt Lou challenged.

"Listen, ladies. I'm the manager here as well as the clerk. We don't want any trouble on these premises."

"Then I judge you don't want any trouble with the law, either?" Eloise Drew reminded him. "Suppose this Mr. Sidney Boyd is involved in a fake stock swindle?"

"*A swindle!*" The manager gulped. "Why—why, I always suspected there was something phony about that fellow Boyd," the clerk stammered. "He's such a glib talker. Such a man with the ladies."

"What does he look like?" Nancy inquired.

"Oh, the usual type," the clerk shrugged. "Small and slender. Dark eyes. Slick patent-leather hair."

"Well, that settles one possibility," Nancy

thought. "Sidney Boyd can't be Mrs. Channing's husband. He's a big, broad-shouldered man. But if Boyd sold fur stock to Mrs. Reynolds, he may have sold some to others in the hotel." Aloud she said, "Would you mind if I question some of your staff about Mr. Boyd?"

The clerk hesitated. "I don't know, Miss Drew. We have a small organization here. Everyone's pretty busy."

"It will take only a few minutes," Nancy pleaded. "I want to talk to the bellhops and porters. And especially to the chambermaid on Mr. Boyd's floor."

"Very well," the man agreed. "Step into my office, ladies. I'll send the bellhops in first."

The bellhops could tell Nancy nothing about Sidney Boyd except that he tipped them generously and never seemed to work. The maids on three floors likewise could add nothing.

It was only when Nancy interviewed Katy, the fourth-floor maid, that the picture, so far as it concerned Mr. Sidney Boyd, began to clear. Katy did not want to talk at first. But Nancy's sympathetic attitude soon drew her out.

"Mr. Sidney Boyd was very particular," the maid explained. "Always wanted his bed made just so and extra towels in the bathroom. He got up late and sometimes, while I was waiting to clean up, he chatted with me friendly like."

"What did you chat about?" Nancy asked.

"Oh, he talked about when he was a little boy in Canada," said Katy vaguely. "He said his mother was French and that his pa was a fur trapper. Mr. Boyd knows a lot about furs," the maid rambled on. "That's how I come to buy some of his fur stock."

"Forest Fur Company stock?" Nancy said quickly.

"Yeh. I had a little money saved up," said Katy, twisting her hands nervously. "Maybe I shouldn't have spent it. But Mr. Boyd felt sorry for me. He wanted to help me make more money. He mentioned big dividends."

"Have you had any yet?" Nancy asked.

"No, but Mr. Boyd promised some money soon."

Eloise Drew could restrain herself no longer. "Why, the man's a contemptible rascal!" she cried out indignantly. "How can he rob hard-working people that way?"

"*Rob!*" Katy exclaimed, tears flooding her faded eyes. "You're saying that Mr. Boyd took my money and—and cheated me?" she wailed.

"I think you'll get it back," Nancy soothed. "We just want to find out—"

Katy had already leaped to her feet. With a hysterical sob, she flung open the office door and rushed from the room.

Nancy's aunt was sorry she had spoken.

"Nevertheless," said Miss Drew, "this sort of thing makes me heartsick. When I think of all the sorrow these thieves have caused, even jail seems too good for them. What do you propose to do next, Nancy?"

"See Sidney Boyd," Nancy answered. "And turn him over to the police."

As she and her aunt approached the hotel desk, they heard the clang of the elevator door and the sharp click of high heels. An agitated voice called:

"Nancy Drew! . . . Wait!"

Bunny Reynolds ran across the lobby toward Nancy. The actress's eyes were wild and her face was chalk white.

"Katy told me everything!" she panted. "It's dreadful! Just dreadful! Fake fur stock!"

"Perhaps you'll get your money back," Nancy said. "At least I'm trying—"

"And the earrings!" the actress interrupted. "What about the diamond earrings I bought from Sidney Boyd? I suppose they're worthless, too!"

CHAPTER IX

The TV Tip-Off

THERE was no quieting Bunny Reynolds. The woman was so agitated that Nancy and her aunt accompanied her back to her room on the fourth floor.

It was cluttered with photographs of herself and other show people. The woman paced the floor. Her eyes blazed as she discussed Sidney Boyd.

"To think how I *trusted* that villain!" she lamented, waving her arms dramatically. "Oh, oh, oh, to think I bought bogus fur stock! I shall punish that unworthy soul!" Cooling off a bit, she added, "And then, yesterday evening, I let him sell me those no-good earrings."

"Earrings?" The word sent Nancy's brain racing. "Are you sure they're no good?"

"Of course I am. If that fur stock is worthless, the diamonds must be too."

"Not necessarily," Nancy said. "Where did he get the earrings?" Nancy asked.

"He said he inherited them from his mother; that he never intended to dispose of them until he met—*me*. That only a woman with fire and artistic temperament should wear them!"

"I must see them!" Nancy thought. Then she said to the actress, "I'm no jewel expert, Miss Reynolds, but would you mind letting me examine the earrings?"

Bunny opened the door of her clothes closet. She stood on a chair and groped far back on the shelf until she drew out a satin slipper. From it she took a rolled stocking, which she unwound to disclose a small velvet box.

"Here they are," she announced. "I haven't even looked inside since Sid—I mean Mr. Boyd—told me to tuck them away safely."

Nancy took the case from Bunny's hands and opened it. *The case was empty!*

Bunny Reynolds let out a shriek. "He stole them!" she cried. "That horrible man took my money and then stole those diamond earrings."

"It looks that way," Nancy agreed, and her aunt nodded. "The diamonds must be real after all."

The actress burst into tears. "I can't afford to lose all that money," she sobbed.

"No, and neither can a lot of other people who have bought Forest Fur Company stock," Nancy said grimly. "Miss Reynolds, what did the earrings look like?"

"They were beautiful. Beau-ti-ful!" the actress sighed. "Tiny platinum arrows, tipped with large sparkling diamonds at each end."

"Platinum arrows?" Nancy suddenly felt sure of her hunch.

She opened her handbag and removed the diamond brooch that belonged to Mrs. Packer. She held it toward the actress.

"Were they anything like this?" she asked.

"Why—why!" cried Bunny Reynolds, "this matches the earrings exactly. Where—how did you get the pin?"

"I'm afraid I have more bad news for you," Nancy said. "The earrings probably are part of a set that belongs to a Mrs. Packer in River Heights. They were stolen from her a few days ago."

"You mean by Sidney Boyd?" The actress gasped.

"I don't believe so. But by someone who no doubt is an accomplice of his. A Mrs. R. I. Channing. Did he ever mention her?"

"No," the woman answered. "But just wait until I get hold of that double-crossing thief Boyd! I'll call the police." Suddenly she brightened. "I have a special friend on the force," she announced, reaching for the telephone. "Sergeant Rolf."

Nancy slipped over to her aunt and spoke softly in her ear. "I'm going to do some investigating, Aunt Lou, and see if I can find out where Mr. Boyd might be," she confided. "Will you stay with Miss Reynolds until I get back?"

Eloise Drew nodded. Nancy crossed the room in a few swift strides. As she flung open the door to the corridor, she collided with the crouching figure of Katy, who very plainly had been listening to the conversation!

"Oh-h, excuse me!" the maid stammered.

Nancy smiled. "Naturally you want to know what's going on, Katy."

"Yes, ma'am, I certainly do," the maid admitted. "Will the police get that awful man, Miss Drew? . . . Will they get him now that he's run away?"

"Run away!" Nancy exclaimed. "Has Sidney Boyd left the hotel?"

Katy pointed mutely to the open door of the room he had occupied. "His bed wasn't slept in last night," she explained. "And all his things are gone."

"Then we must notify the manager at once," said Nancy briskly.

"I've already done that," said Katy. "It's one of the rules. Mr. Boyd checked out of the hotel late last night. The night clerk forgot to tell the manager."

The young detective thought quickly. It was plain what had happened, she told herself. Boyd had sold the diamond earrings to Bunny Reynolds at a pretty price. Then he had stolen them from her. Bold as the man was, he couldn't risk staying in the hotel any longer after that.

The swindler's room was meticulously neat. Nancy went inside and examined it for a clue to his whereabouts but with no success. There was not a scrap of paper in the wastebasket. Nothing of any kind in the dresser drawers nor the desk to give her a clue. Boyd was just as clever as his partner in crime, Mrs. Channing.

While the young detective stood there, the sound of a booming voice in Bunny Reynolds' room announced the arrival of Police Sergeant Rolf. Nancy hurried back to meet him.

The sergeant was a big man with hamlike hands. After hearing Bunny's story, he demanded to see the brooch which matched the stolen earrings.

"If you don't mind I'll take this down to the police laboratory and have some photographs made," he told Nancy after examining it. "Then we can give the pictures to our men and have them watch out for those earrings. Sidney Boyd may try to sell them again."

"Isn't he wonderful!" Bunny cooed, fluttering her eyelashes at the policeman. "You'll get back my money for me right away, won't you, Sergeant?

You'll capture that—that deceitful Sidney Boyd?"

The sergeant looked embarrassed. "Now, Miss Reynolds, give me time," he protested. "Maybe I can have a report for you by tomorrow afternoon."

Bunny rolled her green eyes at him. "Oh, dear, *must* you take that long?" she pouted. "Can't you get some action by tonight?"

Sergeant Rolf fidgeted uncomfortably. "Well —er—the fact is a lot of the men will be pretty busy tonight, Miss Reynolds," he stammered. "It's the Policemen's Ball."

"Oh-h, I see," the actress said in a small hurt voice. "You'll be dancing and having a good time while I—" Bunny's lip quivered and she dabbed pathetically at her eyes.

The sergeant observed her distress and took a deep breath. "Look. I've got no special lady friend," he blurted. "Suppose you come along with me?"

Bunny Reynolds dropped her tragic air like a cloak. "Why, Sergeant—what a delightful idea!" she beamed. "I'd *love* to go!"

Nancy beckoned to her aunt. "I think this is our cue for an exit." She chuckled. "If the sergeant will just write out a receipt for this brooch we'll be on our way."

"Yes, ma'am. Of course," said the policeman. Removing a memo pad from his pocket, he wrote a receipt. "Here you are, Miss Drew."

Nancy slipped it into her purse. She and her aunt left the hotel, turning up their collars against the cold wind.

"You certainly accomplished a lot, my dear," Eloise Drew praised her niece. "And now for the rest of your visit, please let's relax and do no more sleuthing."

Nancy grinned. "At least not until we get a report from Sergeant Rolf," she promised.

"I'm having a special treat for dinner tonight," Aunt Lou went on. "We'll stop at the market and pick up the order."

Her promise of a treat was more than fulfilled. The schoolteacher had been so intrigued by her niece's interest in a fur mystery that she had chosen a trapper's dinner. When the table was finally set with lighted candles and gleaming silver, Nancy heaved an ecstatic sigh.

"Um-m. How delicious everything looks!" she exclaimed. *Venison . . . and wild rice . . .* and my favorite *currant jelly!* Why, Aunt Lou, this is a real north country feast. It's hard to realize we're in New York."

Conversation soon turned to Sidney Boyd and Bunny Reynolds, then to Mrs. Channing and the bogus fur company stock.

"What was it you said about Dunstan Lake?" Aunt Lou asked. "That it was the location of the Forest Fur Company?"

"So it says on the stock certificates," her niece answered. "But nobody—not even the United States Post Office—ever heard of such a place."

"Maybe it's not a town at all." Aunt Lou frowned. "It might refer to a resort without a post office. You know, Nancy, I've heard that name somewhere, but I can't remember when or how. If I only had your sleuthing ability, I'd know in a minute. Nevertheless," she added with a laugh, "I hope you'll always ask me to help you in your mysteries."

"I do call on you whenever I can," Nancy insisted. "Remember how you gave me a hand in *The Clue in the Old Album?* And then there was *The Clue of the Leaning Chimney.* You were simply super in that. And that time you took my dog Togo up to the Adirondacks with you when you closed your summer home, he—"

"Togo!" Aunt Lou interrupted. "I remember now. Someone came to the cottage while we were there. I believe he was a trapper. He was looking for a mink ranch and a Dunstan Lake. But there's no lake by that name around there, Nancy. Perhaps it's the name of the owner of the mink ranch."

"Oh, that's a wonderful clue!" Nancy cried excitedly.

"Please don't follow it tonight," her aunt teased, "or we'll be late for the theater."

Nancy thoroughly enjoyed the mystery drama Miss Drew had chosen. Sunday proved to be another interesting day, and finally when evening came they were ready to enjoy a television symphony concert.

Together, the golden-haired girl and the aunt she so closely resembled seated themselves before the television set in the living room. The musical program was modern and the piano soloist superb. When the show was over, an old film depicting a skating carnival was flashed on the screen.

There was a large picture of the skating queen. Then, one by one, close-ups of her ladies in waiting. Suddenly Nancy leaped toward the television screen.

"Aunt Lou, *look!*" she pointed excitedly. "That tall attendant in the satin robe."

"She's very attractive," Miss Drew commented. "I'd say she's the most attractive of all the skaters. Certainly much more striking than the queen."

"I know her!" Nancy cried.

"Friend of yours?"

"No, no. Aunt Lou, she's the woman I'm trying to find. That's Mrs. R. I. Channing!"

CHAPTER X

The Old Trapper

NANCY and her aunt sat in fascinated silence until the motion picture was over. At the end the cast was named. Mrs. Channing was called Mitzi Adele.

"No doubt that's her stage name," Aunt Lou remarked. "Well, we've discovered she's a professional skater."

"Or was," Nancy surmised. "The film is two or three years old."

"That's right," Eloise Drew agreed. "She may have given up her profession when she married. So I can't see how the information is of much value."

Nancy could not agree. "Now that I know Mitzi Channing was a professional skater," she said, "there must be a lot of people who know where she comes from and something about her background."

"So your problem is to find those people, Nancy?"

"Exactly." Her niece smiled. "Aunt Lou, if it weren't so late, I'd start working on the clue right now."

Soon she and Aunt Lou kissed each other good night and went to bed.

As soon as she and her aunt had finished breakfast next morning, Nancy telephoned the television studio. She asked if anyone there could give her information about the skater Mitzi Adele.

The man to whom she was speaking said the studio knew nothing about her. He advised Nancy to write to the Bramson Film Company, which had made the picture, and ask for information on Mitzi Adele.

"Did you find out anything?" her aunt asked, as her niece put down the phone.

Nancy shook her head. "Only the name of the film company. Oh, I hope they have Mitzi Channing's address!"

Eloise Drew had to leave for school. Nancy said good-bye, for she had decided to take the noon plane. "It has been so wonderful visiting you, Aunt Lou," she said. "And *please,* come to River Heights soon, won't you?"

"On my vacation, perhaps," the teacher promised. "I have one next week."

As soon as Eloise Drew had gone, Nancy sent a

telegram to the Bramson Film Company, asking for a reply to be sent to her at River Heights. Then she packed her bag.

At ten o'clock the apartment buzzer rang. When Nancy answered it, she learned that Police Sergeant Rolf was in the lobby. She invited him to come up.

"I'm here to return that diamond brooch, Miss Drew," he told her, as she opened the door. "If that thief, Sidney Boyd, tries to sell those matching earrings in any store or pawnshop—we'll get him!"

"I certainly hope you do." Nancy smiled. "Won't you step in, Sergeant?"

"No, thanks. I'm on duty," Rolf explained, starting away. "I only wanted to say that the police department appreciates the co-operation you gave us, young lady."

"I'm always glad to help," Nancy assured him. "Good-bye, Sergeant. And the best of luck catching Mr. Boyd!"

At noon Nancy boarded a plane for River Heights. The weather was clear and the flight pleasantly smooth. It seemed as if she had hardly finished luncheon, read the morning newspaper, and solved a puzzle in it, before she was landing at her home-town airport.

When Nancy alighted from a taxicab and slipped into the house, she found Hannah Gruen in the kitchen. Tiptoeing up softly behind the housekeeper, she took a deep breath and called out:

"I'm home!"

"Oh!" gasped Hannah. "How you startled me! Nancy, you must have had a successful trip. I can see it in your face. Take off your wraps, dear, and tell me about it."

"Aunt Lou sent her love," said Nancy as she removed her hat and coat and started for the hall closet.

When she returned, Mrs. Gruen was taking a pie from the oven.

"Oo-oo! *Hot cherry pie!* Hannah, if Bess Marvin knew about this, she'd rush over and—"

"Bess will be here soon enough," Mrs. Gruen replied. "She left word for you to phone her the minute you came in. Call her and then tell me about your trip."

"I'll tell you first." Nancy laughed, and related the whole story.

Ten minutes later she telephoned Bess. The girl excitedly revealed that through a hardware merchant who sold hunting equipment she and George had met another investor in the Forest Fur Company.

"We think you should question him yourself, Nancy," she went on. "The man's an old fur trapper from up North, living with his niece. He's

such a lamb. Reminds me of Daniel Boone. And
—and Santa Claus!"

"Hm-mn. That I must see," Nancy agreed
dryly. "When do we hold this interview?"

Bess consulted George, who took up the extension telephone.

"We'll drive him over tomorrow morning," she
promised. "That is, if we can persuade him to
ride in a car. John Horn doesn't approve much of
'such contraptions.' He's strictly a high boot and
snowshoe man."

Nancy laughed. "In that case, do you recom-
mend I get out my buckskin leggings? And my
coonskin cap with the long tail? But seriously, I
can hardly wait."

"We'll come early," the girls agreed, and
hung up.

Mail for Nancy had accumulated on the hall table. She hastened to examine it. With relief she
found that her duplicate driver's license had arrived. There was also a brief note from her father.
Mr. Drew was eager to have his daughter join him
in Montreal and help him on his case.

As she read, Nancy was conscious of Hannah
Gruen standing near her. "Why don't you open
your telegram?" the housekeeper demanded.

Nancy glanced hurriedly over the table. Then
for the first time she saw the yellow envelope, half
hidden by an advertising circular.

The message was from the Bramson Film Company. It stated that, unfortunately, they did not know Mitzi Adele's address. But a representative of their firm would call on Nancy shortly in regard to the woman skater.

"That's strange," Nancy remarked. "I wonder why the Bramson Film Company is taking all this trouble. It must be something important. I simply can't go to Montreal until I hear what it is."

In the morning the sound of loud voices announced the arrival of Bess, George, and the eccentric fur trapper. Stocky and round-faced, with twinkling blue eyes and a leathery brown skin, the seventy-year-old fellow strode up to the porch with the easy gait of a man half his age.

Watching him, Nancy decided that Bess was right. John Horn was dressed like Daniel Boone, but he had the long white whiskers of Santa Claus. At her invitation they all trailed into the Drew living room and Nancy gestured toward seats around the blazing log fire.

The woodsman declined a chair. He chose to stand directly before the mantel, his legs spread wide apart and his hands deep in the pockets of his leather lumberjacket.

"Well, young woman, I'm here. What do you want to ask me?" he demanded bluntly, his blue eyes boring into Nancy's.

The girl was startled, but she answered him just

as directly. "Is it true that you bought Forest Fur Company stock from a Mrs. Channing?" she asked.

"Yep. I was an old fool," John Horn admitted. "That woman told me what fine mink farms her company had and I leaped to the bait—stupid as a walleyed pike."

"I wonder if she told you anything that would help us trace her?" Nancy persisted, as George and Bess suppressed giggles. "Did she mention a Dunstan Lake, for instance?"

The old man pulled at his whiskers. "No-o. Never heard that name, miss. All we chinned about was mink. You see, I've worked on a mink farm in Canada and I been trappin' the little rascals for years. That's how I come by Arabella, here," he added.

Reaching down into the voluminous pocket of his worn coat, he hauled out a small squirrellike creature with bright black eyes and a long tail.

"Why, it's a *mink!*" cried Bess, running forward to stare at the little animal.

"Sure, she's a mink," John Horn agreed proudly. "Four months old and with as prime a pelt as I ever seen. Notice that glossy dark-brown fur, ladies. See how thick and live-looking the hair is? Arabella's an aristocrat. Yes, sir-ee!"

"Is she tame?" George asked, reaching cautiously to stroke the small alert head.

"She's tame because I raised her myself," explained John Horn. "A wild mink, though, will bite you and his teeth are plenty sharp."

"Where did you get her?" Nancy asked.

"Arabella was born on a mink ranch. The first time I saw her she was pinky white and not much bigger than a lima bean. All baby minks are like that. Very tiny and covered with silky white hair."

John Horn gave his pet a final affectionate stroke and replaced her in his pocket.

"Now I expect we'd better get back to business," he continued. "You want me to help you catch that crook, don't you, Miss Drew?"

Nancy was surprised because she had no such idea in mind. However, if the Dunstan Lake mink farm were located in the Adirondacks, as Aunt Lou believed, it might be very handy to have an experienced woodsman around.

"Mr. Horn, I may need your help if I have to travel up to the frozen country," she admitted.

"You can count on me," said the old man emphatically. "I'll show you how to trap that Channing woman just like I'd trap a mean mink!"

"Excuse me, Nancy," said Mrs. Gruen from the doorway. "I thought perhaps these folks would like some hot chocolate and cinnamon toast."

At the sight of the older woman and her tray, John Horn became, all at once, distrait and ill at ease. "No, thank you, ma'am, I never eat between meals," he said hastily. "Fact is, I gotta **be** goin' right away."

"We'll drive you home," Bess offered.

"No. No. I'd rather walk." The old trapper brushed past the surprised Hannah and out into the hall. Then he turned and came loping back to Nancy, as if ashamed of himself.

"I like you, girl. You—you talk sense," he stammered. *"Here—take this!"*

Suddenly Nancy felt something warm and furry thrust into her hands. The small, wriggling body felt so strange that she gasped and stepped backward, dropping the little mink to the floor.

Instantly, Arabella leaped away, straight toward the astounded Hannah. With a startled cry the housekeeper clutched at her skirts and hopped on to the nearest chair. "Oh!" she shrieked. "A rat!"

"It's only a mink," Nancy said quickly.

She reached down and tried to catch the little animal.

"Don't do that!" Hannah warned. "It'll bite. And the bite's just as bad as a rat's!"

At this moment the little animal scooted directly toward Nancy.

CHAPTER XI

The Mysterious Skier

THE NOISE and confusion that followed the escape of the little mink did not make it any easier to catch her. Arabella, terrified by her strange surroundings and the squeals of Bess and Hannah Gruen, was plainly frantic.

The tiny animal scuttled nervously here and there about the living room in search of a hiding place. Then, in a final burst of speed, she darted through the door and into the entrance hall.

John Horn held up one hand. "Quiet, everybody!" he commanded. "You women there—stay put! *And cut out that yammering!* You'll skeer my poor pet to death!"

There was silence, but Mrs. Gruen still remained standing on the chair. Bess was perched on the arm of the couch.

Nancy and George continued to hunt for the

mink. But it was Mr. Horn who located her crouched in a corner near the front door. The trapper spoke to his pet softly as he approached. Then, kneeling, he took the mink into his arms.

At the same moment there was a quick ring of the doorbell. Nancy opened the door to find a well-dressed man of middle age on the front porch.

"How do you do?" he said. "Perhaps this is the wrong time for me to call. I've been ringing for several minutes."

"I'm sorry," Nancy apologized. "We've just had a little trouble. We were chasing an escaped mink and—"

"*An escaped mink?*" The stranger gave Nancy a stare that suggested her mind might not be completely normal.

Nancy blushed and pointed to the little creature nestled against John Horn's chest. "It's really a tame mink," she explained.

"I see," said the newcomer, but in a tone that showed he did not see at all. Then he added, "I'm Mr. Nelson from the Bramson Film Company. I'd like to speak to Miss Nancy Drew."

"I'm Nancy Drew," she acknowledged. "Please come in." She introduced Mr. Horn, then indicated the high-backed chair near the door. "Would you mind sitting here a few minutes? Then we can have our talk."

Nancy returned to the living room, accompanied by the old trapper. Here, everything was peaceful again.

"I guess I acted pretty silly, Nancy," the housekeeper said, looking very much embarrassed. But, land sakes, I hope you won't keep that squirmy little animal? It gives me the creeps."

"Why, I'd *love* to keep Arabella," Nancy teased, giving her owner a warm smile. "Only I think probably she'd be much happier with you, Mr. Horn. Besides, we have a dog here. That might make trouble."

"It's all right, ma'am," Horn nodded, tucking the little mink back into his pocket. "But my offer of help to catch that thief still goes."

"Thank you," Nancy said. "I'll certainly call on you if I need any."

The two cousins departed with Arabella and her master, who rode away contentedly in the back seat of Bess's car after all. Mrs. Gruen returned to the kitchen. Then Nancy invited Mr. Nelson to join her before the open fire.

The man from the film company wasted no time. "Miss Drew, my company understands that you want to find Mitzi Adele," he said tersely. "Just how close a friend of hers are you?"

"*Friend?*" Nancy gasped indignantly.

In a few sentences the young detective told him what she knew of Mitzi Adele Channing and why various people were so eager to trace her. Mr.

Nelson listened carefully. When Nancy finished, his cold suspicious attitude had vanished and his voice became cordial.

"I'm glad you told me all this, Miss Drew," he said. "Frankly, we thought you might have been mixed up in some of Mitzi's dishonest dealings. My company's experience with Mitzi Channing was very much like your own. We, too, found her to be a thief.

"A few years ago, when we made that picture of the ice carnival, Mitzi was recognized as a talented professional skater. Unfortunately, she took advantage of her position and stole several valuable costumes from the Bramson Film Company. We've been looking for her ever since."

Nancy was not surprised to hear this. She was disappointed, however, that the clue which had seemed so bright was fading out.

"Have you any idea where Mrs. Channing comes from?" she asked.

"Only that her home was in northern New York. Somewhere near the Canadian border, I believe," Mr. Nelson replied.

Since he could be of no further help, the man from the Bramson Film Company took his leave. Nancy was thoughtful. "Every clue I follow seems to lead up a blind alley," the young detective told herself disconsolately. Then she smiled. "Perhaps Dad can give me some ideas. Anyway,

I *must* go to Montreal and help him. He's certainly been patient."

Hurrying to the kitchen, she gave Mrs. Gruen the report about Mitzi Adele, then announced her plans for the trip.

"I believe I'll go this evening, if I can get a train reservation," she said.

Nancy was fortunate enough to secure a compartment on the late express. Then Hannah Gruen helped her pack, slipping in a new pair of navy ski pants, and went with her in a taxi to the station. As the shade-drawn sleepers pulled into the station, she kissed Nancy, saying:

"Now take care of yourself, Nancy. No broken bones on those ski slopes!"

"I promise." Nancy grinned, as a porter lifted her bag aboard.

Next morning, as the train sped through Canada, she could hardly wait until they reached the big snow-encrusted station where she found her father waiting on the platform.

"Nan-cy! I'm so glad to see you!" Mr. Drew cried, and gave her a welcoming hug.

"And that goes double with me, Dad." Nancy tucked a hand beneath her father's arm and walked with him toward a cab stand.

"How goes the great fur mystery?" Mr. Drew inquired. "Have you rounded up those thieves yet?"

"No-o," his daughter sighed. "It looks as if I'm sort of stymied, Dad. I need some advice from you."

"Well, sometimes a change of work helps. Suppose you give me a hand. It will combine business with pleasure. A young man, Chuck Wilson, is the client I came up here to see. I'm a bit puzzled about him. Give me your opinion, Nancy. If you can, get Chuck to tell you about his case himself."

He helped his daughter into a cab which took them to a hotel. Mr. Drew had reserved a room next to his for Nancy. Then father and daughter had a little sight-seeing trip through the snowy city and luncheon in a quaint little restaurant.

"When do I start my work, Dad?" Nancy reminded him.

The lawyer's eyes twinkled. "Don't be so impatient," he chided. "You're going to meet Chuck in approximately one hour. Out at the ski jump of the Hotel Canadien. We'll drive out there."

"Then I'll go back to our hotel and put on ski clothes," she said.

The Hotel Canadien, a few miles out of the city, nestled at the foot of a majestic, snow-covered hill. As Nancy alighted from a cab with her father and approached the foot of the ski run, a jumper was about to take off.

The skier stood far at the top of the hill, his

figure almost dwarfed as he waited for the signal. An instant later he came gliding downward fast as a bullet, only to rise again *high* . . . *high* into the air, soar with waving arms, and then make a perfect landing.

"Good boy!" cried Mr. Drew enthusiastically, as the skier swerved about in a flurry of fine snow and came to a halt not far from where they stood.

"Oh, that was beautiful!" Nancy exclaimed. "If I only could jump like that!"

"Perhaps he'll give you some instruction," said Mr. Drew, smiling. Raising his voice, he called to the skier: "Hey, Chuck! . . . Chuck Wilson . . . Come over here."

"Chuck Wilson?" Nancy gasped.

The slender figure, in a well-fitting black ski suit, turned his head and waved. He glided gracefully over to them, his blond hair gleaming under the band that held it in place.

After Nancy's father had completed introductions, Chuck said, eying her trim ski suit, "You're a ski fan yourself?"

"Yes, I am. But I don't ski very well."

"Perhaps I can give you some pointers," Chuck suggested eagerly. "Would you like to come to the summit and watch the take-offs? It's much more interesting from there."

"That's a good idea," Mr. Drew agreed.

"I'll leave my daughter with you, Chuck. I

must get back to work. Take good care of her."

"I sure will," the young man answered in a tone that made Nancy blush.

Chuck Wilson waited until the lawyer was gone. Then suddenly he seized the girl's hand and pulled her with him toward the ski run.

"I must see this jump," he told her hastily. "That fellow coming down now is a whiz."

The new skier had made a graceful take-off. For an instant, it seemed as if he would outdistance the jump that Chuck had made.

Then something went wrong. The man's legs spread-eagled on landing and one ski caught in the icy snow, throwing him for a nasty spill.

The watching crowd gasped. Above the momentary silence that followed, a spectator, a short distance away from Nancy and Chuck, let out a cry and rushed toward the fallen man.

"Hey, you idiot!" he yelled. *"What will happen to Mitzi if you kill yourself?"*

At the name Mitzi, Nancy straightened. Leaving her escort, she elbowed her way quickly through the crowd and tried to get a closer look at the unfortunate skier. But she was too late. By the time Nancy slipped and slid in the snow to the spot, both the jumper and his friend had disappeared. She turned back.

"What's the matter? Why did you run off?" Chuck asked as he reached her side.

"I'm sorry," Nancy apologized. "I was trying to find someone. Can we go to the lift house at once? Perhaps he's there."

"Okay," Chuck agreed, leading the way.

The lift house was full of skiers but the man who had fallen and the one who had called out were not there. As Chuck fitted her to a pair of rented skis, she asked him if by any chance he had heard the man's name.

"No, I didn't," he answered. "But, say, would his initials help?"

"Oh, yes! Where did you see them?"

"On his skis. Big letters, burned in."

Nancy's heart skipped. "What were they?"

"R.I.C."

"R.I.C.!" Nancy's spine tingled as if someone had put snow down her back! "Could this be Mitzi Channing's husband? R . I. Channing. Had she stumbled on his trail at last? . . . And that other man. Was he, perhaps, Sidney Boyd?"

CHAPTER XII

A Disastrous Jump

CHUCK WILSON chatted cheerfully as he led Nancy up the long slope where they were to begin their skiing lesson. But Nancy's thoughts were far away. She kept wondering about R. I. Channing and whether her hunch about the man was correct. Was Mitzi Channing's husband *really* in Montreal? Was he the mystery jumper?

"Maybe I should have tried harder to find him," she chided herself.

The ski instructor noticed her faraway look. When they reached the top of the slope, he said:

"Time for class! Suppose you take off from here. I want to study your skiing style."

With a quick shove on her sticks Nancy glided away.

"Not bad. Not bad at all!" Chuck called as she completed her trial run. "You have self-confi-

dence and a fine sense of balance. Have you ever
done any cross-country touring?"

"No," Nancy admitted. "But I'd like to learn."

"We can try some jumps tomorrow," her companion said, smiling. "You shouldn't have any
trouble. Now take off again and try not to bear
so much to the left, Nancy. You need more of
what the French call—abandon."

"Abandon?"

"You know—easy does it." Chuck smiled.
"Learn to ride lightly on your skis. To sway
rhythmically at the turns. Rigid muscles and a
stiff back can cause broken bones and bad falls."

When the lesson was over, Nancy turned to her
instructor. "Thanks for everything," she told
him. "Tomorrow I'd like to try some field jumps.
But now I mustn't take any more of your time."

"My time is yours," Chuck said. "I have no
more lessons scheduled for today."

Nancy was pleased. Perhaps she could get
Chuck to forget skiing and talk about himself.
He almost read her mind.

"I'd like to take you out to dinner tonight," he
said, "and perhaps go dancing."

Nancy hesitated. Her father—again the young
man read her mind. "If Mr. Drew would care to
come with us—"

"Suppose I ask him," Nancy replied, pleased
with her first observation of Chuck Wilson.

"Then it's settled," Chuck said. "I'll drive you back to the hotel now and be on hand again at six-thirty. Or is that too early?"

"Six-thirty will be fine," Nancy agreed.

Mr. Drew was pleased when Nancy told him that Chuck Wilson had invited them to dinner, but he said that he would not go along.

"I'd rather have you encourage him to talk without me there," he said. "Sometimes a young man will talk more freely to a girl than to his lawyer. I feel Chuck has been holding something back. See if you can find out what it is."

Promptly at six-thirty Chuck walked into the hotel lobby and greeted the Drews. He expressed regret that Mr. Drew was not joining Nancy and him.

"Your daughter can become a very fine skier, Mr. Drew," Chuck observed. "All she needs is practice."

"I've no doubt of it." The lawyer smiled proudly. "But I guess Nancy will always be better on ice skates than she is on skis. She was fortunate to have had a very fine teacher. I sometimes thought he might encourage her to become a professional!"

"Why, Dad, you're just prejudiced," Nancy protested.

"If you like skating," Chuck spoke up, "how about going to see a contest that's being held here tomorrow night? I'm going to skate. If you could use two tickets—?"

Mr. Drew shook his head. "I'm afraid Nancy and I shan't be here, my boy. Thank you, though. And now, I must leave you two."

Nancy wondered if her father's decision to leave Montreal had anything to do with Chuck. Mr. Drew had said nothing about their time of departure. In any case, she had better get started on her work!

It was not long before Nancy and Chuck were seated in an attractive restaurant.

"Chuck," she said, "have you skated professionally very long?"

"Several years."

"Did you ever hear of a Mitzi Adele?"

"No, I never did. Is she a skater?"

Before the girl could reply, the orchestra started a catchy dance number. Chuck grinned, rose, and escorted her onto the floor.

Nancy had never danced with a better partner. She was thoroughly enjoying it when suddenly Chuck seemed to forget he was on a dance floor. The musicians had switched to a waltz and Chuck became a skater.

He gave Nancy a lead for a tremendous side step backward which strained the seams of her skirt. Then he lifted her from the floor and spun her in a double circle.

"Chuck thinks he's on an ice pond," Nancy thought woefully. "What next?"

He swung around alongside her and they glided arm in arm in skating style around the dance floor. Another twirl through the air, then the music ended. Chuck clapped loudly.

"Nancy, you're wonderful," he said.

Back at the table she remarked that he must have been dancing all his life. Chuck looked at her searchingly a moment, then said:

"My parents were dancers. Would you like to hear about them?"

"Oh, yes."

"They were quite famous, but they were killed in a train crash when I was twelve years old. It stunned me and for a long time I wished I had died too. I had to go live with an ill-tempered uncle. He hated dancing, and would never let me even listen to music."

"How dreadful!" Nancy murmured.

"That wasn't the worst of it," Chuck went on. He explained that only recently he had found out that his grandfather had left him an inheritance, but apparently it had been stolen from him by his uncle, who had taken charge not only of his nephew but of his inheritance as well.

"Uncle Chad had a small ranch in the north country," Chuck went on. "He gave me a miserable time in my boyhood. My only friend was a kindly old trapper. He took me on long trips into the woods and taught me forest lore. It was from him that I learned to ski and snowshoe and to hunt and fish, too. I guess Uncle Chad became suspicious that the old man knew about the money my grandfather had left me and might cause trouble. So he scared him away.

"Later on, as soon as I was old enough, I ran off to Montreal," Chuck continued. "And now I've asked your father to be my lawyer. I want him to bring suit to recover my inheritance."

"Dad can help you if anybody can," said Nancy confidently.

"Yes, I know that. But it's such a hopeless case. I have no legal proof of my uncle's dishonesty, Nancy. My one witness has disappeared."

"You mean the old trapper?" Nancy asked.

"Yes." Chuck nodded. "And there never was a finer man than John Horn."

John Horn! Nancy was startled to hear that a trapper named John Horn was the missing witness. Could there be another such man besides the one in River Heights?

She decided to say nothing to Chuck of the possibility that she knew the one person who could help him. After all, there was no need of arousing false hopes until she had made a definite check.

Three hours later, after an exciting evening of conversation and dancing, Chuck left Nancy at her hotel, with a promise to meet him at the ski lift the following morning. She hurried to her father's room to tell him her discoveries. The lawyer was not in, so Nancy decided to make a long-distance call to her home in River Heights. Hannah Gruen answered the telephone but there was little chance for conversation.

"I can't hear a thing you say, Nancy," the housekeeper protested. "There are two jaybirds chattering at my elbow. I'm so distracted I can hardly think."

"Oh, you mean Bess and George?" Nancy laughed. "Put them on the wire, please."

"Nancy, I'm so happy it's you!" cried Bess an instant later. "George and I came over here because we thought Mrs. Gruen might be lonely."

"Besides, we had a feeling you might call," George put in on the extension phone.

"Tell us what you've been doing. Tell us *everything!*" Bess urged eagerly.

"Well, I had a skiing lesson this afternoon. My instructor was a client of Dad's named Chuck Wilson."

"And what did you do this evening?" Bess persisted.

"Chuck and I had dinner together, and danced, and talked."

"Hypers!" George whistled. "So you're calling him Chuck already."

"And I suppose this Chuck Wilson is young and *very* good-looking?" Bess asked. Nancy could detect disapproval in her tone.

"He is," Nancy chuckled. "But I don't see—"

"I'm thinking of Ned Nickerson," Bess reproached her. *"Don't you break Ned's heart, Nancy Drew!"*

"Nonsense," Nancy countered. "Now listen carefully, Bess. I have a job for you and George. I want you to see that old trapper, John Horn. Ask him if he ever knew a boy named Chuck Wilson."

"We'll do it first thing tomorrow," Bess promised.

Nancy was up early next morning. At breakfast she told her father Chuck's complete story, ending with the item about the old trapper.

"That's a stroke of luck for us." The lawyer nodded. "If your man proves to be our missing witness, Chuck Wilson may really have a case. You've done a fine job, my dear. Are you seeing Chuck today?"

"I'm meeting him at the ski lift at ten."

"Well, have a good time. I'll see you at lunch. By the way, we have reservations on the five o'clock train."

"I'll be ready."

Chuck Wilson was waiting for Nancy at the ski lift. "You're going to enjoy field jumping," he predicted. "And it's a positive *must* if you intend to be a really good skier. One never knows when he'll come to a fallen tree or some other unexpected object. When that happens, the skier must be able to jump or risk a bad smashup.

"Now there's a slope with a sizable hummock at its foot." He pointed. "Suppose we climb up there and have a go at it."

"Just tell me what to do," Nancy urged.

"The first thing to remember is that when you hit a bump it will lift you into the air," her companion cautioned. "Your job is to crouch down before you hit your obstacle. To spring upward and sort of synchronize your spring with the natural lift the bump gives you. Is that clear, Nancy?"

"I think so."

"Good! Then here are a few other rules," Chuck continued as they reached the crest of the little hill. "Try to pull your knees up under your chest as you jump, Nancy. And push down *hard* on your heels so that the points of your skis won't dig into the ground and trip you."

"That's a lot to remember," Nancy replied. "I'd feel better if there weren't so many people milling about the field. When I come down, I want a clear track."

"Oh, you'll be okay," Chuck assured her. "All you need is practice. Well, Nancy, *this is it.*

Take a good grip on your sticks. Get set . . .
GO!"

In an instant Nancy was off. Flying gracefully
as a bird, down the long, smooth slope, she
watched the snow-covered bump ahead of her
loom larger . . . LARGER. And then, suddenly, her heart skipped a beat, and she gave a
gasp of dismay.

An amateur skier floundered directly into her
path, stumbled—and fell! Nancy had to choose
between jumping over his prostrate body or crashing into him.

She must jump!

Nancy dug in her sticks, crouched, and sprang
upward. She came down in a heap.

Chuck Wilson cried out as she spilled, and sped
down the slope to his pupil's rescue.

"Nancy! Nancy!"

The girl lay motionless!

CHAPTER XIII

A Surprise Announcement

"NANCY! Are you hurt?"

The girl opened her eyes dazedly and looked up into Chuck Wilson's worried face. He was kneeling beside her and chafing her wrists.

"W-what happened?" she asked in a faint voice.

"You spilled," Chuck explained. "You made a nice clean jump over that sprawling skier and then—*smack-o*—you pitched on your face. But it wasn't your fault, Nancy."

"Not my fault? You mean that man—"

"He got in your way all right," Chuck answered. "But it was more than that. It was a loose strap on one of your skis." The instructor showed it to her.

Nancy sat up. "I want to try again," she said.

"That was quite a shake-up," Chuck protested anxiously. "Do you think you should?"

"Of course I should."

With her companion's assistance Nancy rose to her feet. "See, Chuck." She smiled. "No bones broken. Nothing injured—except my dignity."

They laughed and climbed the slope together. For the next hour, Nancy practiced field jumps under Chuck's instruction, this time without spills. She was learning so quickly! Too bad it was her last day here, she thought.

"I wish you didn't have to return to the States so soon," the young man grumbled. "Isn't there some way you can persuade your father to change his mind, at least until after the ice show tonight?"

"I think there's a ghost of a chance," Nancy confided, a sudden idea popping into her mind. "At least I have a very good argument."

"Swell! Then I won't have to say good-bye." Chuck beamed. "Here, Nancy, take these tickets to the ice show. I'll expect you and your father there tonight."

"I can't promise," she reminded him, but accepted the tickets in case they could use them. "So long for now, Chuck."

Nancy took a cab back to the hotel and met her father for a late luncheon. "Dad, is it necessary that you go home right away?" she asked. "Couldn't we stay here at least one more day?"

Mr. Drew eyed his daughter with amusement.

"May I ask why? Is it the skiing—or young Wilson?" he teased.

Nancy made a face. "I like Chuck and I enjoy the skiing. But seriously, I'm thinking of the Channings selling more of that fake fur stock, and maybe right here in Montreal."

"What makes you think those rascals are in Montreal?" the lawyer asked.

Nancy told him about the ski jumper she thought might have been R. I. Channing.

"If he's here, perhaps Mrs. Channing is too," Nancy reasoned.

"In that case," her father replied, "I'm willing to delay our departure and give you an opportunity to investigate. Will this interfere with that skating contest tonight?"

"Oh, no!" Nancy cried. "That's part of my plan. Have you forgotten Mitzi Adele Channing is a professional skater?"

Mr. Drew smiled. "Now I'm beginning to see what you have in mind. You think Mitzi may attend the show, that she may even enter the contest, and try for some of the prizes?"

"Exactly." Nancy nodded. "And if Mitzi does show up, then we can call the police and have her arrested. Even if she doesn't come, I may be able to pick up some information about her from the skaters."

The headwaiter suddenly appeared at the

Drews' table. "Pardon me, but are you Miss Nancy Drew?" he inquired.

"Yes, I am," the girl acknowledged.

"There's a long-distance call for you," the man continued. "Please take it from a booth in the lobby, ma'm'selle."

Nancy excused herself and hurried to the telephone. The caller was George Fayne.

"Nancy, we have good news for you," her friend reported. "Bess and I just returned from John Horn's. He remembers Chuck Wilson. And he said that if there is anything he can do to help him, he's more than willing to go to Canada."

"That's just what I wanted to hear," said Nancy excitedly. "I'll be home in a few days. And I'll have a lot to tell you girls."

"Hey, don't hang up," George pleaded. "Have you another mystery on your hands?"

Nancy laughed. "This one is Dad's," she answered. "I'm only helping."

She returned to the table and gave her father George's message.

"Now we're getting somewhere," the lawyer said enthusiastically. "Or at least you are." He smiled proudly at his daughter. "I'll tell Chuck as soon as possible. Meanwhile, what are your plans for the afternoon, Nancy? This old city is full of interesting, historical places. Why don't you look around?"

"I'm going on a hunt for the Channings," Nancy announced. "I can combine sight-seeing with a visit to fur shops and hotels."

Nancy trudged around the picturesque city all afternoon, but did not find a trace of the Channings. Finally, at five-thirty, she returned to the hotel.

Snow had begun to fall, and soon became a wild storm. An icy wind whistled from the north, setting all Montreal to shivering.

"It's a good thing the ice show wasn't planned for outdoors," Mr. Drew remarked, as they waited for a cab under the hotel's marquee.

Traffic moved at a snail's pace so that it was almost eight o'clock before their cab reached the ice arena.

The big auditorium was already crowded with spectators when they entered. Thanks to the tickets provided by Chuck Wilson, the Drews were seated in the center section and well down in front, where it was easy to get a close view of the skaters.

While the band played and the crowd chattered, Nancy studied her program. Chuck Wilson would skate first. No Mitzi Adele was listed as a skater, however. No Mitzi Channing, either. Nancy borrowed a binocular from the man next to her and scanned the audience. The fur stock saleswoman was not a spectator, she decided, after a careful scrutiny.

"I'm afraid we've drawn a blank, Dad," she sighed.

"I wouldn't give up hope too soon," Mr. Drew cautioned. "A thief like Mrs. Channing might be using still another name—or a disguise."

"I wish I knew where to reach a policeman fast," Nancy mused. "If that woman does appear, I'll need an officer in a hurry."

"Then go to one of those little black boxes scattered about the walls," her father said. "They connect directly with a police booth in the balcony. It's all part of their protection system."

"Dad, you're so clever!" Nancy cried admiringly. "How ever did you figure that out?"

"I didn't," the lawyer chuckled. "I called the manager here this afternoon and he told me. Now let's settle back. The show's about to begin."

"ATTENTION! PLEASE!"

Suddenly the blare of the band ceased and a voice boomed out over the loud-speaker.

"*Attention!*" it repeated. "This is to announce a late entry in the Skaters' Waltz. Miss Nancy Drew. Miss Drew will represent the U.S.A."

Nancy's father turned in astonishment to look at his daughter. "Why didn't you tell me you were going to skate?" he asked.

"But I'm not!" Nancy protested. Suddenly she leaped to her feet. "Dad, it's that horrible Mitzi Channing again! She's using my name!"

Nancy's cheeks were flushed with anger as she raced toward the skaters' dressing rooms on the first floor.

"This time I'll find that Channing woman," she told herself angrily. *"She won't get away again!"*

CHAPTER XIV

Flashing Skates

NANCY dashed down the broad stairs of the ice arena two at a time. A sign indicated that the dressing rooms were to the left. But as she headed in their direction, a uniformed attendant blocked her path.

"Not so fast, young lady! Nobody's permitted back there but the skaters."

"But I'm Nancy Drew!" In a flash of inspiration she showed him her driver's license.

The man looked at the name "Nancy Drew" and stepped aside. "I don't understand. I thought Miss Drew came in before," he said in confusion. "You'll find your room straight ahead. Look for your name."

The corridor was crowded with men and women skaters in colorful costumes. Nancy wandered hastily among the performers. She studied

111

the face of each woman in the hope that she might recognize Mitzi Channing. But Mitzi was not there.

Suddenly an eager voice at her elbow asked, "Nancy! Are you looking for me?"

She turned to see Chuck Wilson, very dashing in a black-and-red pirate's suit.

"Oh, no, Chuck, I wasn't looking for you. That is, not exactly," Nancy said.

"Say, what's this about your entering the skating contest?" Chuck asked. "Why didn't you tell me?"

"It's all a mistake," Nancy answered. "I'll explain later, Chuck. There's no time now."

"Very well. Just as you say."

Nancy edged quietly past the dressing rooms until she came to the one with her name on it. Tensely, she raised a hand and knocked. There was no response. Nancy took a deep breath. She turned the knob and entered, closing the door behind her.

The dressing room was empty!

The young detective felt sick with disappointment. To be so near Mitzi Channing, and then to lose her again!

Nancy made a quick survey of the room and everything she saw confirmed her suspicions. Mitzi Channing had been here and very recently. The scent of her unusual perfume was thick in the air. And a hairbrush and bits of make-up lay scattered on the dressing table.

On a chair was the costume which Mitzi evidently intended to wear in the waltz number. It was a white satin dress with a short ballet skirt and a pair of white skating shoes.

Apparently something had scared the woman away. Who could have warned her? Had she seen Nancy come into the auditorium?

The girl returned thoughtfully to the crowded corridor and began to question the skaters waiting here. No one recalled seeing a woman who resembled Mitzi Adele.

Chuck Wilson came over to Nancy. "I have a solo part in the first number," he told her. "I'd like to have you see it. Why don't you go back and watch? There's plenty of time for you to get into your costume. Your number isn't on for forty minutes."

"I'm not going to skate," Nancy answered, "because I'm *not* the girl who signed up for that Skaters' Waltz."

"What!"

"It's a long story, Chuck, but you can do me a favor and answer two questions."

"Okay, if it'll help."

"First, did you speak about me to anyone here? I mean after that announcement on the loudspeaker."

Chuck looked embarrassed. "Well, maybe I did mention to some of the performers that I know you," he admitted. "And I said that you were with your father in the auditorium."

"Where were you standing while you were talking?" Nancy asked. "Anywhere near the door of the room with my name on it?"

"W-why, yes, we were," Chuck replied. "Say, will you tell me what all the mystery is about? I have a right to an explanation."

"Please, Chuck, not with all these people around." To herself Nancy said, "So *that's* how Mitzi found out I'm here! She knew she didn't dare skate under my name after finding out I was here."

"Is Miss Drew here? . . . Miss Nancy Drew?"

The speaker was a short, plump man with a carefully waxed mustache. He stood in the center of the corridor, looking extremely upset.

"That's Mr. Dubois, the manager of this show," Chuck whispered.

"I can give you some information about her," Nancy volunteered.

The man motioned her and Chuck into a room and closed the door behind him. "Speak up quickly, mademoiselle," he urged. "In thirty minutes this skater from the United States must perform. And now I can find her nowhere!"

"I don't think you will find her," Nancy said

calmly. "I'm sure she has left. That woman isn't Nancy Drew at all. That's my name. This other woman is wanted by the police and was using my name. She's Mitzi Channing."

The manager threw his hands in the air. "Nancy! Mitzi! Police! What does it matter to me?" he wailed. "I have a show to put on. She was magnificent."

"Then you know her?" Nancy asked eagerly.

"Yes. No. Listen, girl, don't you accuse *me* of having anything to do with a criminal."

"I'm not accusing you of anything," Nancy replied quickly. "But surely you want to help catch a thief. Please tell me what you know about the skater who ran away."

Mr. Dubois calmed down. He could tell little about the woman, but his description identified her as Mitzi Channing. She and a man had walked into the office during the afternoon and asked for a tryout. From Mr. Dubois' account Nancy was sure she had not heard of the man, who had given his name as Smith.

"They were excellent skaters," the manager said, "so I gave them permission to waltz. Funny thing, the woman wouldn't allow her partner's name to be announced."

"I can understand that," Nancy mused. "Thank you for the information."

A bell sounded. Mr. Dubois and Chuck hurried out, for the show was to begin. Nancy went to a telephone and called the police, alerting them about the Channings and their confederates.

Back in the auditorium, Mr. Drew became more and more anxious as the program continued, and Nancy failed to return. Once, he even considered leaving his seat and going in search of his daughter. But he decided against this.

The lawyer knew that she worked fast when on a mystery case, and he trusted her to act intelligently and keep a level head.

He had assumed that the late entry in the waltz number would be scratched. The lawyer was amazed, therefore, when a second announcement was made that Miss Nancy Drew from the United States would skate next. Her partner would be Charles Wilson.

"Why, that's Chuck!" Mr. Drew gasped, completely perplexed.

He blinked unbelievingly as his client, in close-fitting black slacks and an open-necked white satin shirt, glided out gracefully on the ice. The band had swung into the melodious strains of a waltz. With him was a golden-haired girl in a white satin ballet costume. Mr. Drew's eyes widened in even greater astonishment.

His daughter!

The two skaters danced together in perfect unison, and then spun off on separate tangents.

While Nancy executed some simple steps, her partner jumped and whirled in perfect timing with the music.

All this time Nancy's eyes had been roaming among the spectators, because half an hour before, while Chuck was skating his first number, she had conceived a daring plan. When he returned to the corridor, Nancy had congratulated him, then asked:

"Do you think I danced that waltz well enough with you last night to try it on skates?"

"Why, sure. You're super," Chuck replied. "What's on your mind?"

"There's not enough time to tell the whole story," Nancy said, "but I'd like to take the place of that woman who called herself Nancy Drew."

The girl detective, on a sudden impulse, had figured that by doing this she might get a clue to the runaway skater. One or more of Mitzi's friends might be in the auditorium. Not knowing of her disappearance, they would have stayed.

"When I come on," Nancy thought, "the change will be noticed. One of Mitzi's friends may reveal himself. I'll notify the building police to hold for questioning anyone who tries to leave the building before the show ends."

Turning to Chuck, she said, "Will you skate with me if Mr. Dubois will let me, and if I can borrow a costume and skates?"

"You bet I will." He grinned. "And we'll probably get a prize."

"Oh, no," Nancy said quickly. "I don't skate that well. I—I just want to prove something."

She pleaded with him not to try anything tricky. She would leave the fancy steps to him.

"You're to put on the show," she said. "While everyone's watching you, I'll be doing a little detective work."

"Detective work?" Chuck asked, puzzled. After she had explained her idea to him, he said, "I see. Okay. Request granted." Then he made a face. "I was hoping you just wanted to skate with me."

"I do," Nancy said quickly. "But to tell you the truth, I'm scared to death."

"Nothing to be afraid of," Chuck said cheerily.

Mr. Dubois had been co-operative. Chuck had assured him Nancy was both a good dancer and a good skater. The manager had introduced Nancy to a girl her age and size. Willingly the girl had offered to lend Nancy her skates and an extra costume she had with her.

Despite Chuck's words of encouragement, Nancy's heart had pounded with fright when the loud-speaker had announced their number. But gradually, with Chuck's confident voice guiding her, she had lost her nervousness.

Now, as he glided toward her, and the waltz on skates was about to end, he grabbed Nancy's wrists, swept her from her feet, and spun round and round in a grand finale. When the music blared the last note, he set her down, saying:

"Good girl! Take a bow!"

Nancy was a bit dizzy, but she obeyed. Applause rang in her ears.

As her vision cleared, she noted that a tall, heavy-set man had risen from his seat and was hurrying toward an exit. R. I. Channing, Nancy thought! She turned excitedly to her skating partner.

"Come on, Chuck," she urged. "Let's get back to the dressing rooms quickly. I think the mystery is about to be solved!"

CHAPTER XV

The Password

"Well, here he is, Miss Drew!"

A big policeman thrust his prisoner through the open door of Nancy's dressing room and looked at her.

"We've been watching for this fellow ever since you warned us that he might try to make a get-away," the officer went on.

"He denies everything."

"Of course I deny it," the prisoner snarled, twisting away from his captor's grasp and glaring at Nancy. "My name is Jacques Fremont. I'm a respectable citizen of Canada, and I never heard of an R. I. Channing!"

The man was bluffing, Nancy felt sure. The tall, muscular body, the touch of gray at his temples—all tallied with Nurse Compton's description of Mitzi's husband.

"I suppose you never heard of Mitzi Adele, either?" Nancy asked.

For an instant the man looked startled. Then his eyes locked with Nancy's in a glare of hate. "No, I never heard of her, either," he sneered. "See here, Officer, this is outrageous. I have an identification. Here's my driver's license. It'll show that I'm Jacques Fremont."

The policeman looked at the license in the man's wallet, then nodded. "Everything seems to be in order," he admitted. "I'm afraid that if you have no more proof than this, Miss Drew, we'll have to let the man go."

Nancy was taken aback. She was sure of her accusation. But there was nothing she could do but thank the officer for his trouble and watch as the man who called himself Jacques Fremont slammed angrily out the door.

"If only I weren't in costume and could follow him!" she sighed, then looked up in relief to see her father standing on the threshold.

"Congratulations, daughter!" Mr. Drew called. "I was never so surprised as when—"

Nancy did not let him finish. "Dad! Quick! That tall man you just passed—the one in the brown overcoat. Follow him!" she implored.

"But, Nancy—"

"I'm sure he's R. I. Channing. I asked the police to stop him," Nancy went on rapidly. "But

Channing insisted his name is Jacques Fremont—and they let him go. Oh, Dad, trail him, please!"

"All right, Nancy," the lawyer agreed, dashing off.

Nancy had just put on her street clothes when Chuck Wilson knocked on her door. "I thought perhaps you'd like to go out somewhere for a late supper, Nancy," he invited. "After all that exercise, I'm hungry as a bear."

"I'd like to," Nancy replied. "But I must go to the hotel and see Dad as soon as he gets back. I'll tell you what. Suppose you drive me there and we'll have a bite in the soda shop."

Once they were in the car, Chuck Wilson glanced curiously at the girl beside him. "I suppose I shouldn't ask why you were expecting the police?" he began. "You've shown me there are a number of things you don't care to divulge."

"I can tell you now," Nancy replied. "I'm trying to catch a woman who stole my driver's license and goes around using my name. This evening I tried to have the police arrest her husband. But the man was too clever and they had to release him. Dad went to trail him, though."

"And you can't wait to get the report." Chuck grinned. "I don't blame you. To be honest, I was afraid your secrecy might have had something to do with my case. When the policeman went to your dressing room—"

"Oh, I'm sorry, Chuck. Didn't Dad get in touch with you this afternoon?"

"No. I wasn't at home. Can you tell me what he wanted?"

"I suppose I can. It's good news. Your old friend John Horn has been found," Nancy announced.

"What! Oh, boy, that's great!" Chuck shouted, and yanked the steering wheel hard. In his excitement he had let the car head for a snow pile.

When they reached the hotel, Nancy left word at the desk for Mr. Drew to meet her and Chuck in the soda shop. Half an hour later he came in and dropped wearily in a chair beside them.

"Mr. Drew," Chuck spoke up, "Nancy says you've located John Horn."

The lawyer smiled. "Nancy did," he answered. "Actually, my daughter has done more on your case than I have," he confessed. "But as soon as we get back to River Heights, I'll see this man Horn and have a talk with him about your uncle."

"And what did you learn on *my* case, Dad?" Nancy asked eagerly. "Did you find Mr. Channing?"

"I did—and I didn't, if that makes any sense," her father replied. "Chuck, will you order me a hamburger and coffee, while I start the story? That rascal Channing moves fast—very fast,

Nancy. I spotted him soon after I left you, and almost caught up with him."

Nancy's face fell. "But you missed him?"

"Yes," her father admitted. "The man hopped into a cab. But I did manage to get the car's license number and later located the cabman. He told me that Channing, or Fremont as he calls himself, went to the New Lasser Hotel."

"Oh, Dad, that's wonderful!" Nancy cried triumphantly. "All we need do is watch the hotel and wait for all the thieves to show up there."

"It isn't that simple," her father replied. "I talked to the manager of the New Lasser. He's a fraternity brother of mine and very friendly. He said that a Jacques Fremont, a 'Miss Nancy Drew,' and 'Miss Drew's' brother occupied a suite of several rooms on the second floor. Unfortunately for us, 'Miss Drew's' brother checked out for the trio an hour before I arrived."

"Oh, dear," Nancy groaned, "now we must start hunting for them all over again. Did you get any clues about where they went, Dad?"

Mr. Drew took a bite of his hamburger sandwich, chewed it slowly, and swallowed before answering. Nancy knew from the twinkle in his eyes, though, that he had something important to reveal. Finally he spoke.

"It seems that Mitzi was expecting an important long-distance call at ten tomorrow morning.

When she found she must leave town in such a hurry, Mitzi wrote out a message and entrusted it to the clerk. The message read:

"*'Foxes after stock. Transferring to camp.'*"

"What does that mean?" Chuck asked blankly.

The lawyer and his daughter shrugged, but Mr. Drew prophesied that Nancy would soon learn the answer. Then he changed the subject.

"The performance you two put on this evening was most commendable," he said. "Nancy, I knew you were good on skates, but I didn't know you were that good."

Nancy gave Chuck a sideways look. "I didn't know it, either!" she said.

The gay little party broke up soon afterward. Mr. Drew confessed to being very sleepy, but Nancy remained wide awake for hours. She kept thinking of the message Mitzi Channing had left with the hotel clerk, wondering about its true meaning.

At breakfast she joined her father in the coffee shop with a brisk air that indicated she had come to a decision. With laughter in her eyes, she said:

"Good morning, Dad, you old fox!"

"Fox?" Mr. Drew raised his eyebrows in surprise.

"I was thinking of Mitzi," his daughter explained. "I believe when she wrote that message,

'*Foxes after stock,*' she meant us, Dad.   You and I are the wily foxes."

"That might be," the lawyer admitted.

Nancy confided a daring plan she had conceived before going to sleep.

"Well, good luck," he said when she finished. "But be careful!"

Shortly before ten o'clock Nancy entered the lobby of the New Lasser Hotel, and strolled over to the telephone switchboard operator.

"My name is Drew.   Miss Nancy Drew," she explained, displaying her duplicate driver's license.   "A long-distance call at ten o'clock—"

"But I was told Miss Drew had checked out," protested the operator.   "In fact, the clerk gave me a message to deliver when the call comes in."

"I know," said Nancy.   "I intended to leave town but decided to stay.   I'll just sit here and you can signal me when the call comes through. That is—if it's not too much trouble."

"No trouble at all," said the operator.   "Wait, Miss Drew.   I think your party's on the line now. Take the end booth, please."

Nancy's heart was pounding as she hurried toward the telephone.   So much depended on whether the person on the other end of the line was convinced that she was Mitzi Channing.   Cautiously she lifted the receiver and said:

"Hello!"

"Hello," snapped back a man's brisk voice. And then it added a second word—"*Lake*."

For an instant there was silence while the empty lines hummed. Nancy thought frantically. "Lake?" That must be a password between the swindlers, she told herself. Suddenly a possible answer snapped into her mind. She set her jaw and tried to make her voice sound coarse.

"*Dunstan*," she replied.

CHAPTER XVI

Slippery Sidney

THE WORD "Dunstan" seemed to satisfy the man at the other end of the wire. Evidently convinced that he was talking to Mitzi Channing, he identified himself as Sidney.

"Listen, Mitzi!" he said excitedly, "I've got a deal cooking here for a thousand dollars' worth of stock. That crazy Mrs. Bellhouse will buy it." He laughed softly. "But I've got to work fast and push it while the old lady's in the mood."

"Swell," Nancy murmured in a carefully muffled voice.

"Sure it's swell," Sidney agreed. "But the trouble is, I'm nearly out of certificates. You'll have to get more printed and rush 'em to me!"

"You mean to River Heights?"

"Speak up!" Sidney ordered. "I can scarcely hear you."

"I said—*where* do you want the stock sent?"
Nancy repeated.

"Why, to the Winchester Post Office, of course.
General Delivery," the man snapped. "As soon
as I make this sale, I'll beat it to Dunstan's. I
think we'd better all lay low for a while. G'bye,
Mitzi."

The receiver clicked as the man abruptly ended
his conversation. For an instant, Nancy leaned
against the door of the telephone booth and waited
for her wildly beating heart to calm down.

Her ruse had worked! Now she knew definitely
where one member of the gang could be located.

Nancy hurried from the New Lasser back to
her own hotel. Here she found her father impatiently pacing back and forth in the lobby.

"I'm glad you're here," he said. "Please hurry
and pack."

Mr. Drew explained that he had been called
back to River Heights and that they must leave immediately. He had secured reservations on a
plane taking off within the hour.

There was no chance for Nancy to tell him
what she had learned until they were seated in
the plane. The Drews had taken time, though, to
telephone Chuck Wilson and give him the reason
for their hasty departure.

"Please let me know about John Horn," he had
begged.

"We'll do that," Nancy had promised.

As the plane sped swiftly toward the River Heights airport, Nancy told her father about the mysterious Sidney.

"I'm sure he's Sidney Boyd," she said. "The one who sold stock and earrings to that actress, Bunny Reynolds, in New York. And then stole the earrings from her!"

"Obviously you're right," Mr. Drew agreed. "But if Sidney Boyd is to be trapped, you must supply him with new stock to sell to Mrs. Bellhouse."

"Yes, and that's where I'm stumped," Nancy sighed. "Dad, would it be possible to make copies of the stock from Hannah's certificate and mail them to Sidney Boyd at the Winchester Post Office?"

"Perhaps," Mr. Drew answered. "I know a trustworthy printer who would do a rush job for me. However, as a lawyer, I must warn you, Nancy, that it's illegal to print fake stock even for a worthy purpose. So suppose I telegraph the attorney general and get his permission first?"

The big plane had no sooner landed at River Heights than Nancy and her father departed on their separate ways. The lawyer went immediately to his office. Nancy hurried to a telephone and searched diligently through the books in an effort to locate Mrs. Bellhouse. But without results. Next she went to the public library and thumbed through various directories. She had no luck.

Apparently no one by the name of Sidney Boyd's intended victim lived either in Winchester or in any of the near-by towns. Nancy went home, wondering how she could find the woman.

At dinner her father reported that he had received permission to copy Hannah's stock certificates. And that the printer would do a rush job and have the stock ready by noon the next day. Mr. Drew would rush them to Montreal and have them air-mailed to Winchester.

"I'm glad," Nancy answered. "But something worries me, Dad. I can't find Mrs. Bellhouse's address anywhere."

"Never mind!" the lawyer said cheerily. "As soon as those stocks are mailed, we'll notify the Winchester police. They can watch the General Delivery window at the post office and shadow Sidney Boyd after he takes the package."

"But, Dad," Nancy said, "suppose Mr. Boyd calls for the package under another name? Mitzi might have sent it that way."

"You're right," her father agreed. "And also Boyd might go to Mrs. Bellhouse and collect the thousand dollars. That is a poser."

It was Hannah Gruen who solved the problem. She said that if Mrs. Bellhouse was elderly she probably needed medical attention from time to time. "So why not seek Dr. Britt's aid?" the house-keeper suggested.

"That's a wonderful idea," Nancy said excitedly, rushing to the telephone.

Dr. Britt was as obliging as usual. He had never heard of Mrs. Bellhouse, but he offered to inquire about her at once among his medical friends.

"I'll let you know what I learn, Nancy," he promised.

Next morning Bess and George arrived at the Drew home, bursting with curiosity about Nancy's adventures in Montreal. Seated tailor fashion on the floor in front of the fireplace the three girls enjoyed an hour's confab.

George reported that John Horn had gone ice fishing for a few days on a friend's farm, but as soon as he returned, the trapper wanted to talk to the Drews.

"He says Chuck Wilson's a right handsome lad," George put in.

"And to think that you skated in a contest with him," Bess purred. "Some girls have all the luck!"

"Well, wish that my luck still holds." Nancy smiled. "I hope Dr. Britt can find Mrs. Bellhouse."

At that precise moment the telephone bell rang. Answering it, Nancy recognized the voice of the physician's office nurse.

"I think we've located that Mrs. Bellhouse for you," Miss Compton said. "A Dr. Green recently placed a Mrs. Bellhouse in the Restview Nursing Home, at the edge of Winchester. Visiting hours are between two and three-thirty."

"Oh, thank you," Nancy cried gratefully. "I'll be there on the dot of two."

"Any news about the stock swindlers?" the nurse asked.

"One of them may be caught in Winchester," Nancy replied. "The police are watching for him."

"I'm glad to hear that," Miss Compton said in a tone of satisfaction. "Let me know if any of them are caught, will you?"

Nancy said she would, then hung up. After telling the cousins about the patient who might be the Mrs. Bellhouse she wanted to locate, Nancy announced that she was going to call on her.

"Will you go along?" she asked. When George said, "Wouldn't miss it," Nancy added, "Let's start now. It's a long drive."

On the way she confessed to being fearful that Sidney Boyd might have become suspicious and already have taken the thousand dollars away from Mrs. Bellhouse.

"Oh, don't worry so much," Bess urged. "Maybe she's not the right woman after all."

Just a few minutes before two o'clock the girls

pulled up in front of a rambling, white house flanked on the right side by a grove of birch trees. Nancy rang the bell. After a long wait a uniformed nurse opened the door.

In answer to Nancy's request that she be permitted to see Mrs. Bellhouse, the nurse said that her patient was not able to have any callers that day. She had been ill and was now asleep.

"Could you please come tomorrow instead?" the nurse suggested.

"Yes, of course," Nancy murmured.

Back at the car she told the cousins of her disappointment, but suggested they stay near by to see if Sidney Boyd showed up. Bess groaned at the thought of an hour and a half's wait, but she finally settled back to enjoy the car's radio and a box of crackers.

Of all the callers at the rest home there was not one man, and at last the girls drove home. But promptly at two o'clock the next day the three friends returned, hoping to catch Sidney Boyd. Nancy had learned that he had not called at the Winchester Post Office General Delivery window. And no one who had asked for mail had been suspected by the detective on duty of being the stock salesman.

The same pleasant-faced nurse Nancy had seen the previous afternoon admitted the girls. She led them toward a small but sunny front room on the second floor.

"My patient will be pleased to see you," she informed them. "She loves young people."

Mrs. Bellhouse was a fragile old lady with silvery hair and faded blue eyes. She looked up and smiled as Nancy approached her bed.

"You're very pretty," she said gently. "Do I know your name?"

"I'm Nancy Drew, Mrs. Bellhouse. And these are my friends, George Fayne and Bess Marvin."

"So young—all of you," murmured the invalid. "Did Sidney Boyd send you? Sidney's a relative, you know. The husband of my dear cousin Elsie."

Nancy looked around quickly and saw that the nurse had left the room. "Are you expecting Sidney today?" she asked.

"Oh, yes. This very afternoon," Mrs. Bellhouse nodded. She crooked a finger and motioned Nancy to bend nearer. "I have something for Sidney, but I don't want that starchy old nurse to know," she chuckled. "See, it's right here."

As she spoke, the old lady pulled out a drawer of her night table. Under some tissues lay a crisp pile of currency.

"It's a thousand dollars!" she confided.

Nancy pretended surprise, saying how generous the woman was.

"Not generous at all," Mrs. Bellhouse answered crisply. "I'm buying stock from Sidney in a wonderful mink ranch. The dividends will pay my board here for a long time. I wish Sidney would hurry."

George had posted herself near a front window to watch for the salesman. Presently a car parked and a man alighted. George gave Nancy the high sign, and the three girls said a hasty good-bye to Mrs. Bellhouse.

In the hall Nancy gave quick orders. George was to go downstairs and call the police. She and Bess secreted themselves in an empty sewing room which adjoined that of Mrs. Bellhouse. Here she opened the connecting door a crack, and motioned Bess to silence.

Their retreat was just in time. A dapper-looking man with a pencil-thin mustache came striding into the old lady's room.

"Cousin Clara!" he exclaimed, clasping her hands. "How well you look! Charming! I wish I might spend the afternoon with you, but you know how business is. Well, I've brought you the stock certificates. Is everything ready?"

"Sidney, I've been thinking about dear Elsie," Mrs. Bellhouse quavered. "She never did let me know when she married you."

"Never mind. You've probably forgotten," he said evasively. "Now we must hurry before that horrid old nurse comes back. Have you got the money?"

"It's right here," said Mrs. Bellhouse. "Are you sure that these stocks will give me a big income, Sidney? That I won't have to worry?"

"Of course, Cousin Clara. Now you take the stock," he handed her an envelope. "And I'll take the money. That's it."

While the indignant girls watched the man stuff the bills into his pockets, they heard footsteps behind them. George! She bobbed her head to indicate success, forming with her lips, "Radio police car coming."

As Sidney Boyd started to leave his victim, he cocked his head and listened to the braking of an automobile in front of the house.

The man rushed to a window and looked out. A look of consternation spread over his face and he bolted from the room without a word.

Nancy was already at the door. As she entered the hall, she was just in time to see Sidney Boyd disappear down the back stairs.

"Come on, girls!" she urged. "He's as good as caught!"

BURIED SECRETS ???

CHAPTER XVII

In the Police Net

THE REAR STAIRS in the nursing home were narrow and unlighted. There was a sharp turn halfway down. When the excited girls reached the steps, a door at the foot slammed.

"Boyd's gone!" Nancy thought woefully, groping for the handrail.

The girls raced down the steps. As Bess reached the turn, she tripped and fell against Nancy who was just ahead of her.

"Oh!" Nancy murmured, nearly losing her balance.

George groaned and helped Bess to her feet, saying, "Hold on to that rail!"

The delay gave the fleeing man a good head start. When the girls finally dashed through the back door and onto the grounds, Sidney Boyd was nowhere in sight.

"He's gone!" Bess wailed. "And it's all my fault. I'm terribly sorry, Nancy."

"Never mind the tears," George said, her eyes roaming in every direction. "Where'd that man go?"

"Let's separate!" Nancy advised. "It's the only way to find him."

George dashed around the left side of the house but did not see Boyd. She kept on going toward the front.

Bess raced toward the rear of the grounds to a garage. The thief was not hiding inside, so the girl sped around to the back of it. The man was not there, nor was he running across the field beyond.

Meanwhile, Nancy had made a beeline for the grove of birches at the right side of the nursing home. She darted from tree to tree, and suddenly spotted her quarry crouched behind a clump of saplings.

Sidney Boyd saw her coming. He jumped up and sprinted toward the road.

Nancy, fearful she could not hold the thief even if she caught him, cried out loudly:

"Help! Help!"

She kept on running. The distance between her and Boyd was narrowing.

"Help! Help!"

Her plea had been heard. George, who had

come face to face with the two policemen from the radio car, pointed excitedly and jumped into their automobile.

"Hurry!" she urged. "The thief—Sidney Boyd —he's down the road!   Nancy Drew's found him!"

The driver sped in the direction of the sound. Another cry for help!

"Oh, dear, I hope he isn't hurting Nancy!" George exclaimed worriedly.

Just then they saw Boyd, who now crossed the road and started over an open field.   The police car stopped.   The driver got out and sprinted after the thief.   Within a few seconds he had overtaken him.   When the others reached the spot, Boyd was trying to shake himself free from the officer's iron grasp.

"What's the meaning of this outrage?" he sputtered.

"You'll know fast enough," the policeman told him.   Turning to Nancy, he gave her a quizzical glance.   "Suppose you tell him, miss."

"Who is this girl?" Boyd snapped, giving Nancy a venomous glare.

"Nancy Drew," she replied.   "I'm sure you've heard of me through your friend Mitzi Channing."

The man winced but instantly denied the accusation.

"The New York police are looking for you," Nancy went on.   "Bunny Reynolds wants those diamond earrings you sold to her, then stole."

Boyd's face was livid, and he had become speechless. The policeman told him to march to the car; the conversation would continue back at the Restview Home.

Bess met them on the porch. "Oh, Nancy, I'm so glad you caught him!" she exclaimed. "Now poor Mrs. Bellhouse can get her thousand dollars back. Let's not tell her the stock is worthless. She might have another attack."

"Worthless?" Boyd repeated indignantly. "What do you mean?"

"You know there's no Forest Fur Company at Dunstan Lake, Vermont," George accused him.

A suave smile suddenly spread over Boyd's face.

"If there's anything phony about the Forest Fur Company," he said with an injured look, "that's not *my* fault. I'm merely a broker."

"There's a warrant out for your arrest," said the policeman. "You can tell your story to the judge. But first we're going to call on Mrs. Bellhouse."

While one policeman began a search of their glowering prisoner, the other one went upstairs to get evidence from the elderly woman. When the thousand dollars was taken from the prisoner, Bess asked apprehensively:

"You'll return the money to Mrs. Bellhouse, won't you?"

"Of course," the officer agreed. "And, by the way, Miss Drew, I'd like you to ride back with me. Your friends can follow along in that convertible of yours."

A few minutes later, with Nancy beside the driver and Sidney Boyd handcuffed to Detective Jones in the rear seat, the police car headed for the Winchester Police Headquarters. George and Bess followed in Nancy's convertible.

"You arrived at the nursing home just in the nick of time," Nancy complimented the policeman. "Thanks."

"You deserve most of the credit for this capture, Miss Drew," the officer said. "That's why I'm taking you to headquarters."

Reaching it, Nancy was introduced to the captain, who praised her highly for her fine detective work. After Boyd had been arraigned and committed to a cell in the jail, the captain brought out a photograph from his file.

"Miss Drew," he said, smiling, "since Boyd's case is as much yours as the police's, I think we should share some information one of our men picked up this morning. Boyd never came to the post office—I believe he was tipped off not to—but a letter arrived for him. This is an X-ray photo of it."

The letter, postmarked New York, was brief, but startling. It read:

"Dear Sid:
      Tell Dunstan to come across with
some pay or there won't be any more
stock printed.

                                        Ben"

"It means," the captain said, "that the fur stock is printed in New York, and that Sidney Boyd is definitely one of the gang. I'm going to send one of the stock certificates to the New York police and have them trace that printer Ben."

At this moment the captain's telephone rang, so Nancy thanked him for his help, then went outside to her car.

"Hypers!" George cried. "We began to think we'd have to bail you out."

"And between us, we have only three dollars and fifty cents." Bess giggled. "What *were* they doing to you in there?"

As Nancy drove toward River Heights, she told the girls about the mysterious printer, Ben.

"With Boyd and Ben out of the way, the rest should be easy," Bess prophesied. "Nancy, you deserve a vacation. How about it?"

Nancy's eyes suddenly twinkled. "Good idea," she said. "How would you girls like to go to Aunt Lou's lodge in the Adirondacks? She has a vacation coming up. Maybe she'd chaperon us."

"Oh, but we'd freeze up there!" Bess shivered.

"Poof!" George scoffed. "The lodge has a big

fireplace and think of all the fun we could have
—skiing and bobsledding!''

"Besides," Nancy said, "it's between semesters at
Emerson University. Maybe we could invite the
boys."

At this last suggestion Bess definitely perked
up. Soon the girls were making enthusiastic plans
in which their friends, Ned Nickerson, Dave
Evans, and Burt Eddleton were to be included.

"Look, there's more behind this idea of yours
than just a house party," Bess said presently. "It
has something to do with that fur mystery."

"Could be," Nancy admitted. "Remember
Aunt Lou first heard of Dunstan Lake when she
was at her summer home. It's possible Lake's
camp is in that vicinity."

"And you figure we can do some sleuthing up
there with the boys?" Bess asked.

"Exactly," Nancy admitted. "Suppose you
come into my house while I phone my aunt. I
hope we can start day after tomorrow."

"So soon?" George grinned broadly.

Bess was thoughtful. "What about the boys?
Suppose they can't go?" she quavered. "It
wouldn't be safe up there without some men. I've
heard the Adirondacks are full of bears—"

"Who sleep all winter," George added in disgust.

Nancy laughed. "There probably won't be anything more dangerous around than some minks."

"But I thought you said those stock swindlers—" Bess began.

"No need to worry yet," Nancy advised. "First I have to see about Aunt Lou, and if she can go, then—"

"Then how the wires to Emerson will hum!" George finished.

CHAPTER XVIII

The House Party

NANCY telephoned at once to her aunt. Eloise
Drew readily agreed to lend her summer home for
a house party and she said she never dreamed that
her clue about Dunstan Lake would bring her
such an interesting vacation.

"My hunch may be wrong," Nancy warned.
"But we'll have fun, anyway."

"Suppose you pick me up at the station in York
Village near camp," the teacher suggested. "I'll
arrive there at three-thirty."

Bess and George hung over Nancy's shoulder
as she said good-bye, and then placed a call for
Emerson University. The three boys were enthusiastic about a trip to the Adirondacks. Burt
said they could take his family's station wagon.

"Grand," said Nancy. "But we'd better have
two cars, so I'll take mine, too."

The boys said they could spend only a few days, however, since they had only a short vacation between semesters. This news prompted Bess to pout. When the long-distance conversation was over, she complained, "That's not much time to solve a mystery and have some fun, too!"

Everybody was excited about the excursion to the Adirondacks except Hannah Gruen. The housekeeper predicted accidents on the icy roads and a blizzard that might keep them snowbound. And she expressed her opinion, in no uncertain terms, of "blackhearted scalawags" who cause "innocent young people to risk their lives."

"Mrs. Gruen," she said, "would you feel happier if someone like John Horn was around to guide us?"

"I certainly would," Hannah answered. "And I'm sure your father would too."

That evening Nancy and the lawyer went over to call on the trapper, who had just returned from his ice-fishing trip.

To Nancy's delight, John Horn verified Chuck Wilson's story about his ill-tempered uncle. The trapper told several incidents which had made him suspicious that the elder Wilson was helping himself to certain funds and not making an accounting of them to the Probate Court.

"But I never could prove it," the trapper said.

"You've been very helpful," the lawyer told

him. "And I may call on you to be a witness."

Before the Drews left, Nancy made her request about the trip. The elderly man's eyes glistened.

"You couldn't 'a' asked me anything I'd rather do," he beamed. "But I won't ride in any of them motor contraptions. No sir-ee. The train for me. And I'll mush in from the station at York. I was brought up on snowshoes."

"Your going relieves my mind," Mr. Drew said, and added with a laugh, "Keep my daughter from making any ski jumps after those thieves, will you?"

The trapper chuckled. "Don't you worry. I'll pick up their tracks in the snow and call the police while your daughter's off gallivantin' with the young folks."

Two mornings later the little caravan of young people began its trip. With skis, poles, snowshoes, and suitcases in their cars, and the girls dressed in colorful snowsuits and the boys in mackinaws and fur caps—their outfit resembled a polar expedition.

"Too bad that old trapper wouldn't let us give him a lift," said Ned, as he joined Nancy in the convertible.

"Oh, John Horn's like that. A mind of his own and very independent." Nancy laughed. "When I asked him to help find those swindlers, the old fellow became really excited. Patted his hunting rifle and announced that he intended to 'snare the varmints'!"

For the next three hours everything went well for the travelers. The station wagon followed close behind the convertible. Then, as they reached the foothills of the Adirondacks and began to climb, the roads became icy and the drivers were obliged to decrease their speed to a bare crawl.

Nancy frowned. "I'm worried about Aunt Lou," she confessed to Ned. "Her train reaches York Village at three-thirty and she's expecting us to pick her up."

"York? That's where we buy the supplies for camp, isn't it?" Ned asked.

"Yes, I had hoped to get there in time to shop before Aunt Lou arrives."

At this moment a series of loud toots behind them caused Nancy to slow down and look around. "Oh, dear, Burt's car has skidded into a ditch!" she groaned. "We'll have to pull them out."

It took half an hour and considerable huffing and puffing on everybody's part to haul the station wagon back onto the road. When it was once more on its way, Burt knew that the steering gear needed attention. They must stop at the first town and have it adjusted. Once more he signaled to Nancy and drove forward to tell her.

"You're right," Nancy replied. "Suppose Ned

and I go on and leave the food order at the general store. You pick it up. We'll drive Aunt Lou to camp and start a fire."

Soon the convertible was once more on its way. At the store Nancy ordered ham, eggs, slabs of bacon and other meat, huge roasting potatoes, bread, fresh fruit, and other necessities.

"Friends of mine will call for the order in a station wagon," Nancy explained to the proprietor.

"Come on, we'd better hurry," Ned warned. "I can hear the train pulling in."

He and Nancy dashed to the station, half expecting to see John Horn alight as well as Eloise Drew. But the trapper was not aboard.

"Hello, Ned!" the teacher greeted him, after she had embraced her niece. "And where are the rest of my guests?" she inquired.

"They were delayed," said Nancy. "A little trouble with Burt's station wagon. We're to go on ahead."

"I'm glad we're starting at once," Miss Drew observed. "In an hour it will be dark. And that narrow, snowy road leading to my place can be very hazardous."

Nancy and Ned helped Aunt Lou into the convertible and they began the long climb to the lodge. The road was indeed deep in snow and Ned's driving ability was put to the acid test. All were relieved to see the house.

"Look at that snow!" Aunt Lou exclaimed. "Why, it's halfway up the door."

"Are there any shovels in the garage?" Ned asked, as he clambered out of the car.

"I think so," Miss Drew answered.

Ned struggled around the corner of the house to the garage. He came back swinging a shovel and started clearing a path. Soon the station wagon arrived.

"Reinforcements are here," the boys announced.

In a few minutes they were carrying in the suit· cases. The girls and Aunt Lou followed, shiver· ing in the huge but icy living room.

"We can soon have some heat," Aunt Lou said, taking swift charge of the situation. "Boys, there's plenty of wood in the shed out back. Suppose you start a roaring fire in the grate."

"Girls," said Nancy, "let's bring in those gro· ceries from the station wagon."

"Groceries?" Bess gaped.

Suddenly Nancy's heart sank. "Bess! George!" she gasped. "Didn't you remember to stop for the food? Didn't Burt tell you?"

The blank consternation on her friends' faces was answer enough.

Tired and hungry, the campers had to face it. *There was no food in the house!*

CHAPTER XIX

The Fur Thief

"CHEER UP!" Aunt Lou encouraged her guests. "The situation isn't too black. I left a few canned staples in the pantry here. If you don't object to beans—"

"Beans! Oh, welcome word!" cried Bess, rolling her eyes ecstatically. "I'm ravenous enough to eat tacks."

"Then you'll have to earn your supper," George said firmly. "Get a mop. This place must be cleaned up before we eat."

It was in the midst of their tidying the cottage that a knock came on the door and John Horn walked in. The old fellow looked rosy and fit after his long trek on snowshoes. He explained that he had come up the day before and was camping out in the hills Indian style. When they told him of their predicament about food, he appeared merely amused.

"Shucks, nobody need go hungry," he chuckled. "I shot some rabbits on the way. I'll bring 'em in and give you folks a real treat."

So, thanks to the beans and John Horn's truly delicious rabbit which he cooked himself on a spit in the fireplace, everyone felt satisfied and content. Then, gathering around him, Aunt Lou and her guests listened for two hours to the old trapper's yarns. Later, when Nancy asked him if he had found out anything about Dunstan Lake, he shook his head.

"Nope. Nobody I met ever heard of the man, Nancy. Nor of that Forest Fur Company, either. But they do say there's three mink ranches around here owned by other folks."

Suddenly Eloise Drew snapped her fingers. "I just recalled that the first time I heard the name Dunstan Lake was early last summer at the Longview Inn. I was leaving the dining room when I overheard a woman mention the name."

"Maybe he was selling her some stock," Nancy spoke up. "I think I'll go over there right after breakfast tomorrow and speak to the manager. I'd like to hike over. Could I make it on snowshoes, Mr. Horn?"

"Oh, sure—that is, if you got good muscles, and you look as if you do. Well, folks," the trapper said, rising, "I'll be on my way."

He would not accept a bunk with the boys and

went off whistling in the darkness. The house-party guests rolled wearily into bed and slept soundly.

Next morning, the prospect of a second meal of beans for breakfast had little appeal for the campers. At Nancy's suggestion the young people trailed down to the frozen lake, resolved to try some ice fishing.

The boys hacked a hole in the ice fifty feet from shore and carefully lowered several lines with baited hooks. But although they waited patiently, there was not a bite.

"I guess we'll eat beans—and like it," George groaned.

"Hal–loo there! What you doin'? Lookin' for a walrus?" called a voice from the shore.

They looked around to see John Horn standing there with a heavy pack on his back. The old trapper explained that he had risen before daylight and gone down to York Village.

"I brought back your grub." He grinned. "Wanta eat?"

"Do we!" cried Burt, dropping the line he was holding. "I'll swap an uncaught fish for a stack of hot cakes any day!"

The others echoed his sentiments as they rushed to join the trapper and relieve him of the food. With a grin he set off, saying the time to catch criminals was before they were awake.

Directly after breakfast Nancy and Ned fastened snowshoes to their hiking boots and set out for Longview Inn, five miles away. The snow was crisp and just hard enough for firm going. Shortly before noon they arrived at the entrance to the big resort hotel.

"What a grand spot for winter sports!" Nancy exclaimed, gazing admiringly at the high ski jump and the numerous ski runs and toboggan slides.

"Sure is," Ned nodded. "I wish we had time to try 'em. But I suppose you want to find out about that mysterious fellow, Dunstan Lake. Well, where do we begin our investigations?"

"Pardon me. But would you two be interested in purchasing tickets to our charity contest?" a strange voice inquired.

The couple turned to face a smiling elderly woman. She went on to explain that the tickets were for a skiing party the next afternoon, to be followed by a trapper's dinner at the inn.

Ned was just about to say that they could not make it, when Nancy surprised him by telling the woman that they would take seven tickets! Ned dug into his pocket for the money, but he asked, "Why did you do that?" as he and Nancy entered the hotel.

"Sorry, Ned, I'll pay for the tickets."

"That's all right, Nancy, but maybe the crowd won't want to come."

"I was thinking of Mitzi Channing," Nancy said. "If she's in the neighborhood, she might show up."

"You're right.   Well, let's call on the manager."

Mr. Pike had been with the inn for five years, but he had never heard of a Dunstan Lake.   Nor anyone named Channing, either.   He promised, however, to make inquiries among the guests and to let Nancy know.

When they left the hotel, Ned said eagerly, "Let's go over and look at that super ski jump."

The ski jump was truly spectacular.   A long, smooth runway with a skating pond near its foot. And, right at the edge of the ice, two mammoth figures had been carved out of snow.

"Aren't they wonderful!" Nancy cried out.

As she and Ned stood staring at the snow giants, Nancy felt a hand on her arm.

"Nancy Drew—this *is* a surprise!" said a familiar voice.

"Why, Chuck Wilson!" gasped Nancy.   "What are you doing here?"

"Pinch-hitting as a ski instructor." Chuck grinned.   "The regular pro has a broken leg. And now tell me what you're doing here."

Nancy introduced the two young men, then told Chuck about the house party at her aunt's camp.

"Oh, Chuck, I have a grand surprise for you!" she added.   "Guess what!   John Horn's here!"

"Here!" The skier looked incredulous. "At your camp? I'll be right over!"

Ned looked none too pleased at this suggestion. It seemed to give him great pleasure to say that Chuck would have to look elsewhere for John Horn.

He lost his glum look, however, when Chuck insisted upon lending the couple skis and suggested that they try a few field runs. For the next half hour Ned and Nancy enjoyed themselves on the snowy slopes.

"Nancy, your skiing has certainly improved," Ned said, smiling.

"The credit for that goes to Chuck." Nancy was amused at her escort's sudden change of expression to one of hurt.

Below them, Chuck Wilson waved his hand. "Hey, why don't you try that low jump?" he called.

"I'm game," Nancy cried, pushing off with her sticks. "Come on, Ned!"

Nancy went first and cleared the fence nicely. Ned followed but his was by far the higher and the longer jump.

"Well, at least I didn't spill." Nancy laughed as they pulled up alongside the ski instructor. "And now I think we'd better start back to the camp."

"Nancy, I'll see you again, won't I?" Chuck pleaded.

"We're all coming over here tomorrow," she promised. Then, with a teasing glance at Ned, she added, "But there's no reason why we can't see more of each other today. Ned and I haven't had lunch, so why don't you join us in the dining room?"

"Thanks, I will. But let's go downstairs to the snack corner."

Nancy and Ned returned their borrowed equipment, and Chuck checked his skis and poles at the long rack outside the beam-ceilinged room, crowded with skiing enthusiasts.

Their appetites whetted by a morning in the crisp mountain air, the trio ate heartily. When they finished, Ned and Nancy insisted they must leave, instead of joining the group which lingered by the fireplace to discuss Telemarks and Christianias.

Outside, as they were fastening on their snowshoes for the long hike back to camp, Nancy turned to Chuck. "By the way, do you know where any mink ranches are located around here?"

"There's one up on that ridge where the run for the ski jump starts. A Mr. Wells owns it."

"Then let's go home that way," Nancy suggested to Ned. "We may pick up some information about the Forest Fur Company and Dunstan Lake."

They rode up on the lift and trekked off along

the ridge. Half a mile farther on they came to the ranch buildings. A man started running toward them.

"Did you meet anyone or see anyone leaving here?" he asked excitedly.

"No," Ned replied. "Is something the matter?"

"I'll say there's something the matter," the man growled. "Some of my finest mink peltries have been stolen!"

CHAPTER XX

Racing a Storm

STOLEN!

An idea clicked in Nancy's mind. Could the person who had taken the peltries from Wells' ranch be one of the Forest Fur Company gang? Perhaps even Dunstan Lake?

"Did you lose many minks?" Nancy asked Mr. Wells.

"About two thousand dollars' worth," the agitated man replied. "Half my 'take' for the year."

"Pretty tough," Ned remarked. "When were they stolen?"

"I'm not sure. Just a few minutes ago I noticed the door of the storage house was half open."

"Did you see any new tracks in the snow?" Nancy inquired.

"Come to think of it, I didn't. We had quite a blow here early this morning. The snow could have filled up the tracks."

"Perhaps the furs were taken last night," Nancy said. "I hardly think a thief would prowl around in the daylight. May we see where you kept the peltries, Mr. Wells?"

"Certainly."

The man led Nancy and Ned to a small building attached to the back of his house. As they approached the half-open door, Ned remarked:

"There are only one set of footprints. They must be yours, Mr. Wells."

Nancy leaned down to examine the snow. With her glove she lightly brushed some of it away. The evidence of another man's prints was vaguely visible below the light snow.

"I'm sure your peltries were stolen last night," Nancy surmised. "I wish we could follow the thief's tracks."

Ned looked at her quickly. "You're not going to try brushing away all this snow!" he cried.

Nancy smiled. "If I thought it would help catch the thief, I'd try it."

Mr. Wells let out a moan. "Now I'll never catch the thief," he said. "My peltries are probably in another state by this time."

"We'll try to find them for you," Ned offered. "Nancy is a detective."

"You!" Mr. Wells stared at the girl. "Well, I'll be jigged!"

Nancy wished Ned had not told him, but said

she would do all she could. She asked him if he had ever heard of the Forest Fur Company, the Channings, or Dunstan Lake.

"No, never have," he replied.

Nancy did not explain further. Instead she asked, "Have you notified the police about the theft?"

"No."

"Then I'll do it for you," Nancy offered. "I'd like to speak to them, anyway. Where's your telephone, Mr. Wells?"

The rancher led them into his small house. Nancy noticed that for a man who lived alone, his place was very neat. The living room contained rustic furniture, and a fine, large deer head hung over the fireplace.

"Here's the telephone," he said, pointing to a hall table.

Mr. Wells and Ned entered the living room, and Nancy telephoned the barracks of the State Police. After identifying herself as the niece of Eloise Drew, she reported the theft at the Wells ranch. Then she told about the Forest Fur Company gang and the arrest of Boyd.

"I believe men named Channing or Dunstan Lake may know something about the theft," she said.

The trooper was grateful for the information.

"We'll comb the countryside for the thief, Miss Drew," he promised. "And, by the way, drop in to visit us some time. We'd like to meet a girl detective!"

Nancy said she would and hung up. She returned to the living room to find Mr. Wells pointing to the deer head and telling Ned how he had shot the animal in a near-by woods.

Ned was impressed. "I sure would like to shoot one, so I could hang the head in our fraternity house at Emerson!"

The ranch owner winked at Nancy. "It's yours, son, if Miss Drew nabs the fur thief!"

"I'll do my best," the young detective promised. "Mr. Wells, I've heard a lot about mink ranches but never been to one before. May Ned and I look around a bit?"

"Glad to show you," the rancher replied. As they stepped outside, he glanced at the low, dark clouds which were rolling in from the north. "Looks like more snow," he observed.

"Then we mustn't stay long," Ned spoke up. "We have quite a hike home."

Mr. Wells led them toward one of several small shedlike buildings which set back some distance from the house, and the group went inside. It was about six feet wide and had separate pens on either side of a central aisle. In these pens were some fifty, glossy little creatures which some day would make luxurious scarfs and coats.

"They're beautiful," Nancy remarked. "But they must require a lot of care, don't they?"

Mr. Wells shook his head. "Not a mink, Miss Drew. All he needs is a clean, cool place where there isn't too much sunlight. And, of course, the right kind of food."

"Sounds like a good business." Ned grinned.

"It is, for an outdoor man," the rancher replied. "Anyone who wants to start a successful mink farm should start with the finest, healthiest animals he can buy. And he should establish himself in a cold climate, so that the fur will grow thick. In the United States that generally means the states of Maine, Vermont, New Hampshire, Massachusetts, or northern New York."

"What do minks eat?" Nancy asked.

"So far as feeding goes," the man went on, "that's no problem at all. A mink likes lean meat and fish especially. But he'll eat table scraps and vegetables, too—even field mice. Fact is, it costs less than five dollars a year to feed a mink!"

"Mighty interesting," said Ned. Glancing at the sky, he added, "Nancy, I think we'd better start back. It gets dark quickly up here. And we don't want to be caught in a snowstorm in the dark."

Nancy agreed they had better not tarry. As

they trudged back toward Mr. Wells' house to put on their snowshoes, Nancy suddenly pointed to a small, dark object half hidden under the snow crust.

"It may be a clue to that thief," she said excitedly. "He might have dropped it."

The rancher, who had walked ahead of the couple, did not see Nancy walk quickly toward the spot. Ned followed close behind her. Perhaps she was right. If the fur thief had dropped just one clue, it would help a lot.

Now Nancy was directly over it. She bent down to pick the object from the snow when Ned yelled:

"Don't touch it!"

He gave Nancy a sudden shove, which sent her reeling away from the object.

"Why, Ned!" she exclaimed.

"It's a trap, Nancy!"

By this time Mr. Wells was running back toward them. "Don't touch that!" he shouted. "It's a fox trap."

"Oh!" Nancy exclaimed. "Thanks, Ned. I'm glad you recognized it."

The rancher explained that marauding foxes sometimes approached the mink pens and that he had to keep traps set for them.

"We don't want to catch you, though." He chuckled. "We'll have enough trouble snaring the fur thief!"

When the young people had their snowshoes on again, they said good-bye to Mr. Wells and started off. Ned urged speed because a brisk wind had come up and the dark clouds were rolling in faster.

"Let's go along behind all the mink sheds," Nancy suggested. "If the thieves did happen to leave any clues, we might pick them up."

"Okay."

Behind the sheds, Mr. Wells had planted a thick row of evergreens to serve as a natural snow fence for his property. Nancy and Ned followed along the edge of this barrier, scanning the ground hopefully.

Just by accident Ned happened to look up, and there, wiggling from a shoulder-high branch, was a strand of white yarn.

"This time I think I've found something, Nancy. See if you agree."

As quickly as Nancy could make it on the snowshoes, she plowed over to the tree.

"Agreed, Mr. Detective," she chuckled. "Any further theories?"

"Since you ask," Ned answered, with a bow made clumsy by layers of warm clothing, "I have. Anyone trying to keep out of sight against the snow would wear white. Probably a sweater he could slip on and off easily. Maybe our man did just that, and snagged his shoulder on these thick trees."

"Let's see if we can find any more," Nancy suggested, crashing through the evergreen fence just under the scrap of wool. "I'll follow this side. You take the other."

The evergreens led into dense wood. From time to time, the couple found similar bits of wool caught on tree branches, but then the woods gave way to open ground, dotted only with knee-high clumps of berry bushes.

Ned sighed. "Well, there goes that clue."

The brisk wind that had started back at the mink farm hit them with full force as they emerged from the trees into the open. The bitter cold stung their faces.

"We'd better make for camp in a hurry," Nancy advised. "It's going to storm."

They turned to follow their tracks back to the mink ranch and the trail to Aunt Lou's. The pair was dismayed to find that the wind-blown snow had blotted out their tracks in the woods.

"Seems to me we came from over there, a little to the right," Nancy called to Ned. "Shall we try it?"

"Let's accelerate," he ordered, taking the lead. "Pick 'em up and lay 'em down fast!"

Neither spoke as they raced along. The daylight was growing dimmer by the minute. For two long, arduous hours, the pair tried this direction and that toward home as they pressed on in the face of the rising storm.   Then Nancy called:

"Ned!   Do you know where we are?   We should have reached the camp long ago."

"No," he replied grimly.   "I don't want to worry you, Nancy, but I'm afraid we're lost!"

CHAPTER XXI

An S O S

For several seconds neither Nancy nor Ned spoke. Each of them was trying to figure out how to get back to the cottage before the storm.

Ned sheltered his eyes with one hand and peered through the rapidly falling dusk. All he could distinguish at first were rolling stretches of snow-covered landscape. The lost snowshoers might have been in the arctic wastelands. Then Ned spied a lean-to and they hiked to it.

"Wood!" he exclaimed, seeing a pile of logs in one corner. "I'm going to build a fire. That may attract someone's attention."

"And we can eat," said Nancy. "I have two chocolate bars in my pocket."

The crackling fire and the candy revived their spirits, though no one came to guide them out of the snowy wilderness. Finally, when the fire died down, they set off again. Their journey was down-hill, which at this moment seemed the easiest to take.

"I have a flashlight," said Nancy. "I'll blink an S O S. *Three short, three long, then three short.* Right?"

"Right." Ned agreed.

Nancy clicked the signal several times as they crunched along. Again they had just about given up hope of help, and were floundering in a snow-bank, when Ned said:

"Listen! I thought I heard a shout."

Nancy glanced quickly over her shoulder. "You're right!" she cried. "There *is* a man over there. It's John Horn!"

The trapper came plunging toward them through a drift. "I saw your distress signal, folks," he yelled. "You lost? Why, Nancy! Ned!"

When Ned explained that they were indeed lost, the old man looked hurt. "You should 'a' asked me to guide you," he reproached them. "But, anyways, I can show you a short cut through the woods. You can get home before it snows."

"You're certainly a lifesaver," Nancy said grate-fully. "As a reward, I'll tell you some good news. Chuck Wilson is staying at the inn! We saw him this afternoon."

"You don't say!" Horn exclaimed, his leathery face spreading into a delighted grin. "Well, I'll sure have to tramp over there sometime and visit with the boy."

He started off, with Nancy following and Ned bringing up the rear. Presently the girl noticed that the trapper had about a dozen beautiful mink peltries strapped to his knapsack. She admired them, then asked where they had come from.

"Oh, I picked 'em up," John Horn answered vaguely. "They're the best mink there is!"

Nancy developed a worried frown as she tramped silently behind the trapper. Twenty minutes later they came to a well-defined trail, marked with the stompings of many feet.

"Just follow this trail," said their guide, "and you'll come to your camp. So long, I'll drop over tomorrow."

As the couple watched their rescuer's sturdy figure vanish into the night, Ned said, "Nancy, you look upset. Surely you're not afraid we'll be lost again?"

"No, it's not that," she replied. "I was wondering about those valuable peltries John Horn was carrying, and the ones that were stolen from Mr. Wells."

"Good grief! You don't think that old man's a thief, do you?" Ned demanded.

"I hate to think it," Nancy admitted. "He could have set a lot of traps, I suppose, and had some luck."

Ned shrugged, then said if Horn had stolen the peltries, more than likely he would have hidden them. Nancy agreed, saying:

"I guess I'm so tired and hungry that my suspicions are getting the better of me."

The trail led almost directly to the back of the cottage. "We've been going in circles," Ned remarked ruefully, as they climbed the porch steps. The snow had just begun to fall.

They were welcomed by a frantic group. Aunt Lou had been chiding herself for letting the couple go off without a guide, and actually wept with joy to see her niece and Ned.

Again there was supper before a blazing fire, while Nancy and Ned recounted their adventures. The prospect of attending the big ski party at the hotel aroused all the young people's enthusiasm. They agreed to follow Aunt Lou's advice and retire early in preparation for the big day.

Nancy was so weary that she tumbled into bed like a rag doll. It seemed as if her head had barely touched the pillow when she heard her aunt's voice.

"Nancy! Wake up!" Miss Drew urged. "It's a lovely, sunny day. And there's a telegram for you, dear. A boy just brought it from the village."

"Read it to me, please," mumbled the sleepy girl.

"Very well." Her aunt hurriedly slit the envelope and scanned the teletyped lines. Then she read the message aloud: " 'Nancy, phone me from Longview Hotel. Love, Father.' "

"Aunt Lou, I don't understand," Nancy said, now fully awake and sitting up in bed. "Why should my father send me a telegram like that?"

"Perhaps he has learned something that will help you solve this fur mystery," her aunt suggested.

"Perhaps. But why should Dad ask me to phone from the hotel instead of the village? And why would he sign the message 'Father' instead of 'Dad,' as he always does? Aunt Lou, it looks as if that telegram might be a fake."

"Oh, dear," said Aunt Lou, "those thieves have probably found out you're here. Well, that settles it. No more trips except in a group. And I'm going to phone your father myself from the village."

When Nancy entered the living room a short time later, she found George and the three boys busily waxing their skis. "We've decided to go to the party on skis," Ned explained. "The snow's just right, and we'll work up a better appetite for that trapper's dinner." He grinned.

"Dinner?" Nancy asked. "How about breakfast?"

"We've eaten, sleepyhead," George replied.

Nancy prepared bacon, eggs, and toast for herself. She had just finished eating, when Bess came running in, her cheeks flushed with excitement.

"Listen, everybody!" she cried out. "Someone's been snooping around this house! I saw a lot of strange tracks."

The others rushed outside. In the new-fallen snow there were indeed a series of footprints encircling the house. A man had been both peeping and eavesdropping!

The young people trailed the tracks away from the cottage and on down to the edge of a small grove. Here they disappeared as mysteriously as they had begun.

Where had the eavesdropper gone and who was he?

Back at the cottage, an ugly possibility reared itself in Aunt Lou's mind. The fur stock gang had learned of Boyd's arrest and wanted to get revenge on Nancy! Also, they would stop at nothing to keep her from tracking them down.

Miss Drew felt the responsibility for her niece's safety weighing heavily on her. Nancy must be protected. It was only a matter of time before the mysterious eavesdropper might return, not to observe, but to strike!

CHAPTER XXII

The Hidden Cabin

DISAPPOINTED not to have found any trace of the eavesdropper, the boys and girls returned to Eloise Drew's cottage and made plans for going to Longview Inn.

"I'm driving to the village with Aunt Lou," announced Bess. "We'll meet you at the hotel for lunch."

To Nancy her aunt said, "Anything you want me to tell your father?"

"I guess you know everything I've found out," her niece answered.

The teacher recommended that the skiers start out at once, since it would take them until noon to reach the inn.

A few minutes later, as the five enthusiastic hikers were about to set out, John Horn strode up, a telegram in his hand.

"Did you get one of these this morning, Nancy?" he asked. "Woman over to the telegraph office in the village sent a boy out with one, but he never come back and she wondered if he got here."

"Yes, he did," Nancy answered, opening the envelope.

The message was only a duplicate of the first one. Nancy told John Horn about the mysterious eavesdropper and requested him to go with her and look at the spot where the tracks ended.

"What became of the man?" she asked as they reached the place.

John Horn bent down, then chuckled. "The fellow used the old Injun method of covering his tracks," he said. "He just walked backward and brushed the tracks away with a broom made of an evergreen bough. I dare say he wouldn't keep this up for long, though. Maybe you can pick up his tracks some distance along."

Nancy went back for her skis, then the whole group set off for the inn, watching carefully for any sign of more footprints. At Nancy's suggestion the trapper trailed along.

"This powdery snow will be perfect for the games this afternoon," said Dave. "I hope we can— Hey, gang! Look at that circle of ski tracks just ahead."

"That's queer," said Ned. "It looks as if two or three people met here and—"

"And had a conference," Nancy finished. "Listen, I'll bet that eavesdropper had skis."

By now they had all stopped and were staring down at the crisscrossed lines.

"I think we should investigate," said Nancy. "These tracks seem to split up in three directions. I suggest we separate and see where they go."

"You going to make us deputy detectives?" Burt grinned. "Just give the orders."

"Okay. Dave, will you follow the tracks leading to the hotel? You can see it from here. If you find our eavesdropper, try to nab him!" Dave winced. "Anyway, tell Aunt Lou and Bess the rest of us may be delayed."

"George and Burt, will you swing right toward the Wells ranch?" She pointed. "Ned and I will take that left trail into the woods. And, Mr. Horn, I'd like you to come with us, if you will," she added, smiling at the trapper.

"Sure, I'll come," he agreed. "But I know what you'll find, Nancy. There's a cabin up there but nobody in it. And it don't look natural."

"What do you mean by natural?" Ned asked.

"I mean it's locked tight and boarded at the windows," the old man explained. "The right kind o' woods people allus keep their cabins open for the use of other hunters."

The ski tracks led to the cabin, but did not stop there. The trail ended a hundred feet beyond, where the skier had continued on foot. His prints did not match those at Aunt Lou's cabin, however, so Nancy gave up following them, and turned back.

When the trio reached the cabin, they halted to look at it. The building was small and well screened from the trail. It was tightly locked, as John Horn had said. It was evident from the telltale tracks which stopped at its door that several persons had approached the cabin recently.

"Probably hikers who used it for a spot to rest," Nancy conjectured.

"The cabin may belong to a summer resident," Ned remarked. "Of course he would have locked it up."

"But he didn't put that padlock on the door," Nancy pointed out. "That's brand new!"

"You're a smart girl, Nancy," John Horn nodded. "Reckon I won't go to the hotel yet. I'll just stay here and scout around a bit. You folks run along."

Nancy and Ned pushed off, and twenty minutes later they came to the Longview Inn. It was crowded with sports enthusiasts. George and Burt hurried across the lobby to meet them and reported that they had discovered nothing of consequence. Neither had Dave.

Aunt Lou had a look of concern, however. She beckoned her niece to one side.

"Your father and I are worried about you, Nancy," she said. "He didn't send that telegram!"

"It was a fake, then," Nancy said. "Who *did* send it, I wonder."

"Some enemy did," her aunt replied. "Someone who wanted to make sure you would be at the inn today. Oh, I'm so afraid he intends to harm you. Nancy, you will be extra careful, won't you?"

"Of course I will," her niece promised. "But I'm not in any danger really—not with so many friends about."

Nancy was not deceiving herself. Many times before, when trailing lawbreakers, the girl detective had thought she was safe, only to learn later that her enemies had put her in great danger. By this time the Channings must know that Nancy was responsible for Boyd's imprisonment. They naturally would try to get revenge for this!

"I mustn't fall into any of their traps!" she thought.

Aunt Lou did not look upon the affair lightly, either. She ate hardly any luncheon, although the meal in the hotel dining room was a gay occasion for the young people in her group.

Chuck Wilson appeared while they were eating dessert and Nancy introduced him to Miss Drew and her guests. At Aunt Lou's invitation the ski instructor joined them at their table and he promptly pulled up a chair beside her niece. Presently he said:

"Nancy, you haven't taken your eyes off that door for a moment. Anything wrong?"

"I've been watching the guests as they enter," Nancy confided, "hoping that either Mitzi Channing or her husband might wander in. But no luck so far."

"I've been inquiring around, too," said Chuck. "I'd give a lot to help you solve this mystery, Nancy."

When luncheon was over, a bugle announced the opening of the ski games. Everyone hurried out either to watch or to participate in the contests.

"I'll have to leave you now, Nancy, and get on the job," Chuck explained. "See you later."

The master of ceremonies stood on a platform in front of a loud-speaker.

"*Attention, ladies and gentlemen!*" he said. "It gives me great pleasure to welcome you all here this afternoon. I am glad to announce that five hundred dollars has been collected for the worthy charity to which you have so generously donated.

"To open the program, the management is proud to present a special feature. Chuck Wilson, our new instructor, will make an exhibition jump from Big Hill!"

There was a murmur of anticipation from the

spectators as all eyes turned to the top of the slope where the blond young man stood poised for the leap. Then, at a blast from the bugle, he was off!

"Oh, I hope he makes it!" Nancy found herself thinking, and held her breath.

Chuck raced down the incline, then soared gracefully into space, his arms spread out like a great bird's wings. For an instant, he seemed to hang in the sunlit sky. A moment later he came swooping down, to land gracefully and glide over the level snow.

The watching crowd burst into applause. "Wow! That was something!" Burt Eddleton cried. "I'd give up college any time in favor of learning to do that!" He grinned.

Nancy's crowd skied over to congratulate Chuck. On the way her eyes darted from person to person. Mitzi Adele and her husband were not there.

Aunt Lou, who also had come out to speak to Chuck, whispered to Nancy that she thought it would be best if the girl did not enter any of the games.

"Your name may be announced," she said, "and that's just what your enemies are hoping."

Nancy agreed. She took off her skis and handed them to her aunt, then went to give Ned an explanation. Although he was greatly disappointed about losing his partner, for her own protection he said he would find another girl to enter the next event with him.

Five minutes later the master of ceremonies announced a two-legged ski contest, and gave the names of the contestants. The last couple named was Ned Nickerson and Eileen Smith.

"I'm glad he found someone," Nancy said to Aunt Lou.

Her relative nodded. "Only it's a shame you have to miss all the fun, Nancy."

Her niece squeezed the woman's hand. "It's fun to catch criminals, too!" she said, an impish look on her face.

The two-legged race was designed strictly for laughs. In it, six couples climbed a small hill, where each man and girl removed one ski, the man his right ski, the girl her left. Then with their arms locked about each other's shoulders, they slid down the slope with their free feet in the air.

The object was to reach level ground without falling or touching the free foot to the ground. But before it was over, there was a merry mix-up. Nancy was pleased when George and Burt went the farthest distance and so had won the prize. Ned and Eileen were runners-up.

"All ready for the water bucket race!" boomed the announcer. "In this race each skier will take off with a bucket of water in his right hand. At

the end of the hill, the bucket must be swung once
in a circle. And the contestant who spills the least
amount of water wins!"

Nancy left Aunt Lou and pushed her way
among the milling groups. She saw nothing but
smiling, happy skiers. Not a sign of any sinister
character present.

"I'm probably all wrong," she thought. "I
might just as well have gone into the games.
Sometimes this detective business—"

"Psst! Nancy!"

The voice came from behind her. She whirled
to face John Horn. The old man's eyes sparkled
with excitement.

"Follow me!" He beckoned with a calloused
finger.

CHAPTER XXIII

A Weird Light

NANCY looked anxiously about in hopes of seeing either Ned or another of her friends. But none of them was in sight. Meanwhile, John Horn continued to tug impatiently at her coat sleeve.

"I tell you we got to hurry, Nancy," he pleaded. "She's over on that pond in the woods right now. And skatin' around bold as you please!"

"Who's skating?" Nancy demanded.

"Why, that woman who sold me the fake fur stock," the old trapper snorted. "That thievin' Mrs. Channing, of course!"

At the name Channing, Nancy hesitated no longer. "Lead the way!" she urged.

An instant later the two were running across the hotel grounds. They headed into the woods at the rear of the inn and raced through the snow for nearly a quarter of a mile.

"There she is!" Horn pointed out, as they slowed down and cautiously approached a small, cleared pond.

Nancy felt a tingle of excitement run down her spine. She stood on tiptoe for a better view and craned her neck. Mitzi ended a series of figures directly facing Nancy.

The tall, slender brunette suddenly realized she had been discovered. Like a flash she shot back toward the far bank. Without removing her skates, she raced among the trees.

"Fool!" said John Horn. "She'll probably break an ankle."

He was already unfastening snowshoes from his back, and just as quickly fastened them onto his boots.

"Looks like it's goin' to be a race," he observed. "You follow as fast as you can, Nancy."

He soon outdistanced Nancy, who had tried sliding across the ice to save time. But she had fallen twice and wasted precious minutes.

Some distance ahead, the trapper saw Mitzi. She was seated on a log and had just finished changing into hiking boots. She leaped to her feet and fled farther into the woods, but the old trapper was gaining with every step.

Nancy found their trail and sped after them as fast as she could through the deep snow. Suddenly she heard a scream, followed by:

"Let me go!"

A moment later she came in view of Mitzi and the trapper. She was kicking and scratching as John Horn held her firmly by one arm. The woman's eyes blazed with anger.

"I'll have you arrested for this!" she panted.

"Oh, no, you won't, Mrs. Channing," called Nancy, running up. "We're going to turn *you* over to the police."

Mitzi glared. "Why, if it isn't little Miss Detective herself!" she sneered. "And what have I done?"

"A great deal, Mitzi Channing. You've been selling fake stock certificates and you've stolen furs and jewelry. That should be enough."

"That stock is perfectly good," Mitzi snapped. "And I've never stolen *anything*. If this big gorilla will just . . . let . . . go!" she added, trying to twist away from the trapper's grasp.

"Where's your husband?" Nancy demanded. "And where's Dunstan Lake?"

"Wh-at?"

The startled woman flung back her head. As she did so, her cap, loosened by her struggles, fell to the ground, disclosing a pair of sparkling earrings. They were shaped like small arrows with diamonds at each tip.

"Those are Mrs. Packer's stolen earrings," Nancy charged. "I recognize them."

"They are not. They're mine," Mitzi defended herself. Then suddenly she clamped her lips tightly together and refused to say another word.

"Nancy, there's a couple o' state troopers at the hotel," said John Horn. "If you'll hurry back and get 'em, I'll march our prisoner along and meet you halfway."

"I'll bring them as fast as I can," Nancy promised, and started off on a run.

Nancy planned to tell her aunt and the others about the capture, but she met the troopers first and decided to wait until the prisoner was in custody. She told her story quickly and led the officers toward the spot where she had left the prisoner and John Horn.

But when they arrived, there was no sign of Mitzi Channing. Only the limp body of John Horn, lying unconscious on the snow with a large welt behind one ear.

"Oh!" Nancy cried in horror, and knelt beside him.

One of the troopers reached into his pocket for a tiny vial, nipped off the end, and held the spirits of ammonia under John Horn's nose. Meanwhile, the other officer was inspecting the ground. He said that what had happened was plain. Footprints indicated that the trapper had been overpowered by two large men. Mitzi had vanished into the woods with her rescuers.

Fortunately, John Horn was not badly hurt and revived within a few minutes. He explained that he had been jumped from behind and had had no opportunity to see his attackers.

"But I think I can identify those men," Nancy told the troopers. "One is named Channing, alias Jacques Fremont. The other must be Dunstan Lake."

One trooper immediately set out to trail the men, while his partner hastened off to dispatch a radio alarm. Nancy and John Horn walked back slowly to the inn.

The old man protested that he was all right and that he "needed no coddlin'." But Nancy insisted that he take a room at the hotel and have the house physician examine his injured head.

Eloise Drew and Nancy's young friends were greatly upset by the incident. They concluded the Forest Fur Company gang must be pretty desperate. Nancy called Trooper Headquarters, but there was no word about Mitzi or the men.

Chuck Wilson was deeply concerned over his old friend and spent nearly an hour in John Horn's room. Because of this he almost missed the special dinner the hotel was serving.

The guests enjoyed it immensely. Along with the huntsman's menu, the management had provided a hillbilly orchestra, which played old-time ballads and toe-tingling polkas. Afterward, the tables and chairs were cleared away for a series of square dances.

Nancy swung gaily through the "grand right and left," then promenaded with Ned as her partner. When it was over Chuck Wilson came to join them.

"I'm going upstairs to see how old John is feeling," he said. "Do you folks want to come?"

"Oh, yes," Nancy answered.

They found John Horn pacing the floor of his room like a caged bear. "The Doc won't let me git outta here until mornin'," he grumbled. "He must think I'm a softy."

"Nothing of the sort," Nancy replied, and added affectionately, "You probably saved my life, Mr. Horn. If I'd been standing guard over Mitzi, those men might have carried me off and dropped me down some snowy ravine."

"Don't talk like that!" Ned said severely.

While she had been talking, Nancy had walked to a window to gaze at the beautiful moonlit landscape. Suddenly her attention was caught by a glimmer of light along the ridge at the top of Big Hill. A moment later she could see the steady beam of a flashlight moving rapidly toward the ski run. It seemed very strange at this hour.

"Boys," she called, "why would anyone be up near the high jump at night?"

"I can't imagine," said Chuck, as he and Ned

joined her at the window. "Come on! Let's find out!"

Within a matter of seconds the three young people were waving a quick good-bye to the trapper and hurrying downstairs to the checkrooms. Hastily changing to ski clothes, they raced outdoors.

For a moment there was no sign of the light. Then suddenly it showed up again at the top of the ski run and came hurtling downward, as the unknown jumper soared expertly at the take-off and landed below with a soft swish and a thud.

"Good night!" Chuck cried. "What a chance he took! Let's speak to him!"

He and Ned raced off into the darkness, for already the light had disappeared and a cloud had cut off the moonlight.

Nancy waited until the cloud passed over, then tried to spot the jumper in the moonlight. She could not see him.

"Where could he have gone?" she asked herself. "That man wasn't just a phantom. He was flesh and blood!"

She turned toward the lake and the two giant snow statues which marked the end of the ski jump. Nancy's heart pounded at the sight she saw.

By a mere flicker of light that glowed, then vanished like a firefly, she could detect the shadowy outline of a crouching figure huddled behind the nearer statue. The person was cramming a bulky pouch into a hollow of the snow man!

Nancy opened her mouth to call Chuck and Ned, when a rough hand was clapped over her face.

"Quiet!" a harsh voice commanded. *"And don't try to run away or you'll get hurt!"*

CHAPTER XXIV

Zero Hour

THERE was no escaping from the man's iron grasp, Nancy knew. With her captor's fingers firmly gripping her arms, she had to stand helpless, while the other man ran over from the statue, stuffed a handkerchief roughly into her mouth, tied her hands behind her, and bound her ankles together. Then the two men carried her swiftly toward the woods.

"If only Ned or Chuck had seen me!" the distracted girl thought. "Here I am with friends so close by and I can't even call for aid."

Although Nancy could not see the men's faces, in a few minutes she was able to identify her abductors for they began to talk freely.

"Say, Jacques, how much farther is it to that cabin?" the shorter of the pair asked.

Jacques Fremont! The man whose other name was Channing!

"Only a little ways," he replied. "All we need do is dump the Drew girl inside and lock the door. The place probably won't be opened again until summer."

"What a relief to have her out of the way," growled his companion. "We had an airtight racket until Miss Detective began snooping around, asking for the Channings and Dunstan Lake. Although how she found out *my* name, I'll never know."

"She's clever," Channing admitted. "But too clever for her own good. Now Miss Nancy Drew is going to pay for her smartness.

"Well, Lake, here we are. Suppose we see if this girl detective can solve the mystery of the locked cabin with both her hands and feet tied," Channing continued with a harsh laugh.

The cabin was bitterly cold, even worse than out-of-doors, Nancy thought, as her abductors flung her down on a bare cot. Then, in the glare of a flashlight, Dunstan Lake, a squarish man with a bulldog face and beady eyes, made the girl a mocking bow.

"Good-bye, Miss Drew," he smirked. "Happy sleuthing!"

"Come along! Let's get out of here," Channing snapped impatiently. "It's time we picked up Mitzi at the camp. She'll be tired of waiting."

Nancy shivered and closed her eyes despairingly

as she heard the door slam and the padlock snap. She struggled to get out of her bonds, but it was useless. Already her fingers were becoming cold. With every passing minute the cabin became more frigid. Nancy wondered desperately how long she could survive.

She knew that her only hope lay in exercise. She raised and lowered her bound ankles as high as she could until she was puffing with exhaustion. As she rested a moment, the fearful cold took possession of her again.

Nancy decided to try rolling on the floor. She managed to get off the cot, and in doing so loosened the gag in her mouth. Crying loudly for help, the prisoner waited hopefully for an answer. None came.

She rolled, twisted, and yelled until she was bruised and hoarse. Finally her voice gave out completely, and her strength was gone. She became drowsy, and knew what this meant. Her body was succumbing to the below-freezing temperature!

Meanwhile, back at the slope, Ned and Chuck had completed a futile search for the mysterious jumper and were now walking to the spot where they had left Nancy. "I can't figure why that fellow took off at night," said Chuck. "He could be arrested, you know. It's against all regulations."

"It was probably some crackpot who wanted to

prove how brave he is." Ned shrugged. "Say, Nancy's gone."

"I wouldn't worry." Chuck smiled. "She probably became chilled and went back to the hotel."

"Not Nancy!" Ned retorted. "She *never* gives up! If Nancy's not here, it's for a good reason. She probably spotted one of those swindlers she's been looking for and is trailing him alone!"

Nevertheless, the two young men sprinted to the hotel to find Nancy. She had not come in, Bess reported, and wanted to know what was going on.

"Tell you later," Ned called, as he and Chuck dashed off.

When they reached the ski slope, Chuck cried out, "Look, somebody's coming down Big Hill again! Two men with flashlights."

"But those fellows are descending like sane men," Ned observed. "They aren't taking any jumps."

The newcomers were state troopers. They said they were searching for the thief who again had stolen some mink peltries from the Wells ranch. Chuck told them about the foolhardy jumper and they shook their heads in disgust. The men were about to go on when Ned stopped them.

"Have you seen a girl in a red coat?" he asked. "She was out here with us when we were looking for that crazy skier. Now she has disappeared and

I'm afraid that she's trailing the same thieves **you** are."

"Thieves?" the troopers echoed.

"Certainly thieves," Ned went on. "The girl **is** Nancy Drew, the one who captured that swindler, Mitzi Channing, this afternoon. But the woman got away."

"I heard about that over the police radio," one of the men said. "We'd better help you hunt for your friend. She may be in danger."

"We haven't much chance of trailing anyone," the other remarked. "There's been such a crowd around here, the place is full of tracks. How long has it been since you saw the young lady?"

"About twenty minutes," Chuck answered.

"Then she can't be far away," said the younger trooper. "Why not divide our forces so as to cover as much territory as possible?"

It was quickly agreed among the four that Chuck would search the hotel grounds while Ned followed the shore line along the lake. The two troopers would examine the surrounding woods.

"Let's arrange a signal," said one of them. "The first man to find the girl will turn the beam of his flashlight toward the sky and wave it in an arc. In case of emergency, he will blink the light rapidly until help arrives. Is that clear?"

"Perfectly," said Ned impatiently. "Let's go!"

The next hour was torturous for the hunters.

The heavy snow made the going difficult, and a keen, arctic wind developed that knifed through their stout woolen clothing and sent the tears down their smarting cheeks. Added to this, their spirits were becoming low.

No one found a trace of Nancy Drew!

At the end of the hour the four met. The troopers went back to their headquarters to report, while the two boys returned to the hotel. A frantic Aunt Lou and the remainder of her house party rushed to meet them at the door.

"Where's Nancy?" Miss Drew demanded. "When none of you came back for the dancing, we all became worried and tried to find out what happened. But nobody knows a thing."

In a few minutes the two boys had told the story of the strange skier and their separation from Nancy. Everyone listened in shocked silence. Then Bess offered a ray of hope.

"If John Horn is still upstairs, why don't we get his advice?" she suggested. "He knows more about the woods than all of us."

"Say, that's a great idea," Chuck agreed, rushing to the stairway. "I'll ask the old fellow—" The rest was lost as he bounded up the steps.

In no time he was back. With him was John Horn. The bandage on the old trapper's head was awry. He looked pale, but he insisted upon joining them in a new search.

"If those swindlers nabbed Nancy Drew, they wouldn't 'a' dared take her far off," he said. "I'll bet they took her to that empty cabin in the woods. Yes, sir. That's where they've left her. It's the only place around here where they could hide her without bein' found out."

"Oh, why didn't I think of that?" Ned chided himself, starting for the door. "If anything happens to Nancy—"

"Hold on!" Dave objected. "Burt and I are fresher and we can strike out faster. George and Bess can follow us with a thermos bottle and a blanket. But you and Chuck are in no shape to go."

"What do you mean?" Ned glared. "Maybe I can't go quite so fast, but what if there's trouble? I want to be there to help!"

"So do I," Chuck said firmly.

Nancy's friends hurried through the night, determined to make a rescue.

CHAPTER XXV

The Tables Turned

JOHN HORN kept up as long as he could, then directed the others how to go. Dave and Burt, the first to reach the cabin, yelled Nancy's name. There was no answer.

Eagerly they charged up to the door. When they failed to open it, Burt said:

"Flash your light here, Dave. Padlocked, eh?"

"We'll try a window," Dave suggested. "If necessary, we'll break the glass."

"Hey, is she there? Have you found Nancy?" George called, as she and Bess came hurrying up to join them. Chuck and Ned were close behind.

"We don't know yet," Dave said. "This door is locked. We're going to try getting in a window."

"They're boarded up," Ned recalled. "But we'll get inside if I have to tear this shack apart."

George was using both fists to hammer on

the unyielding door. *"Nan-cy!"* she shouted. "Nancy, it's George. Can you hear me?" There was no response.

Meanwhile, Burt and Dave were working on a window. "Here's a loose board," Burt yelled excitedly. "Pull!"

Snap! It came off so quickly they nearly lost their balance.

Burt flashed his light inside the cabin. He could not see much in the clutter of furniture.

Dave was already pulling at another board. Together the boys yanked it off and broke the locked window just as Aunt Lou came up.

"Nancy!" she called fearfully, but the hoped-for response did not come. By this time Ned was through the opening and flashing his light around.

Suddenly the beam found the girl, lying on the floor, numb with cold and barely conscious.

"Nancy!" Ned cried.

"I'm—so—glad you—found me," she replied faintly. "I'm—so—terribly—sleepy."

One by one the others climbed through the window. Seeing Nancy, tears streamed down Bess's cheeks. "You're—you're all right, aren't you?" she sobbed, as Ned and Dave untied the ropes that bound Nancy's hands and ankles.

"Of course she is," George told her cousin.

Aunt Lou kissed her niece, whispering, "Don't

worry, honey.   We'll get you out of here right
away.   George, where's that thermos bottle?"

Nancy was given a few sips of the bracing drink,
wrapped in the blanket, and carried out through
the window.   Burt and Dave insisted upon riding
Nancy back to the hotel on a "chair" they made
from interlacing their fingers.

A sense of relief, together with the stimulant,
brought some warmth back to Nancy's body.   As
the group neared the inn, she was able to talk
again.

"As soon as we get inside," she said, "call the
police.   Tell them it was Channing and Dunstan
Lake who kidnaped me."

"We guessed as much," George said.   "But
don't talk now.   Save your strength."

"I must say this much," Nancy persisted.   "Tell
the police that those men were going to meet Mitzi
at a car somewhere.   Mr. Lake's a short, ugly fellow with beady eyes."

"I'll tell them," Ned promised.

Aunt Lou would not hear of Nancy's making
the long trip to camp.   Instead, she engaged a
room for her niece and asked Bess to spend the
night with her.   Nancy was put to bed, and Miss
Drew called in the house physician.   After he had
prescribed treatment, the doctor remarked:

"You had a narrow escape, young lady, but

you'll be all right in the morning. Lucky you knew enough to keep exercising, or you might have frozen to death."

Nancy smiled wanly, and very soon was sound asleep. When the girl awoke next morning, Bess, fully dressed, was seated beside her, and a breakfast tray stood on the bureau.

"I'm so glad you're awake," she said. "How do you feel?"

"Fine. All mended." Nancy hopped out of bed. After washing her face and combing her hair, she sat down to enjoy some fruit, cereal, and hot chocolate.

"Are you all set for some simply marvelous news?" Bess asked.

"You bet. Don't keep me in suspense."

At this moment there was a knock on the door, and Aunt Lou walked in with George. They beamed to see the patient fully recovered, and said the anxious boys were waiting downstairs.

"I was just going to tell Nancy the big news," Bess said. "Listen to this, Nancy: the police have captured the Channings and Dunstan Lake!"

"Honestly? Oh, that's great! I was so afraid—"

"The troopers found their camp," George interrupted. "Nancy, do you realize what this means? That you've rounded up the whole gang, just as you hoped to do."

"With the help of all of you, including the state troopers," Nancy was quick to say. "Did Mitzi and the others confess to everything?"

George shook her head. "They won't own up to one single thing. Hypers! The way that Channing woman plays innocent makes me furious!"

As Nancy continued to eat, Aunt Lou remarked, "This place is full of excitement. The Wells Ranch was robbed again last night."

"What! Oh, my goodness!" Nancy cried.

She suddenly thrust the breakfast tray off her knees and jumped to her feet.

"That experience I had last night must have frozen my brains," she wailed. "Why, I've forgotten the most important evidence of all!"

"What evidence?" George wanted to know.

"The snow statue. Bess, hand me my clothes, quick! And, George, bring the boys up here in five minutes. There's not a moment to lose."

When the youths arrived, Ned demanded to know what all the excitement was about.

Nancy took a deep breath. "I'll tell you, Ned. Remember when you and Chuck and I saw a man ski down Big Hill and wondered why?"

"I sure do. He was crazy."

"Maybe not so crazy as you think," Nancy replied. "When you and Chuck left me, I saw the man conceal a bulky pouch in one of those big snow statues."

"You did?" Ned cried. "Nancy, why didn't you mention—"

"I was so cold and tired I forgot about it until just now," Nancy confessed. "Let's run down to the lake. Oh, I hope the pouch is still there!"

Before they could leave the room, the telephone rang. Aunt Lou answered.

"It's the police station, Nancy. They want to speak to you," she said, handing over the instrument.

"Miss Drew, this is Chief Wester," came a man's voice. "We have those three suspects in jail, but they're a hard-boiled lot and refuse to admit a thing."

"I can identify them," said Nancy confidently.

"I know you can point out the men as your abductors," said the police chief. "But Mrs. Channing demands her release and we haven't any charge against her."

"Just call Mrs. Clifton Packer at River Heights," Nancy advised. "The diamond earrings Mitzi Channing is wearing were stolen from her. And the police at Masonville will tell you that Mitzi is wanted there for shoplifting."

"Thanks. You've helped a lot," said the chief. "And, Miss Drew, will you come down to the police station and be present when we question the trio again? I haven't told them that you were rescued."

"I'll drive over this morning," Nancy promised.

She repeated the conversation to her friends and added, "Now, about the snow statue. I suspect that the Channing fur racket, which hasn't been cleared up, will be revealed in about ten minutes."

"How?" Bess asked, wide-eyed.

"When we see what's in that hidden pouch. Why, where are the boys?" she asked, starting out the door.

Aunt Lou smiled and put a restraining hand on her niece's arm. "They're acting as your deputies, dear. Let's sit here quietly until they return."

It was hard for Nancy to wait, but she knew her aunt wanted her to take it easy for a while. Twenty minutes later they heard pounding footsteps in the corridor and the boys burst into the room.

"We found it!" Dave cried.

"Yes sir-ree! Mission accomplished!" Ned said, grinning and waving a bulky, canvas-covered bundle at Nancy.

"Open it!" Bess urged. "I can't wait to see what's inside."

Tensely, the little group gathered around, while Nancy loosened the cord and peered within.

"Furs!" George gasped. "Why, it looks like mink."

"It is," Nancy nodded, pulling several soft lustrous peltries from the bag. "We must turn these over to the police at once. I believe they belong to Mr. Wells."

Nearing the bottom of the bag, Nancy gave an exclamation of glee. To one of the peltries was sewed a small tag, reading *Wells Mink Ranch.*

"Oh, Nancy, you've done it again!" Bess shrieked.

The girl detective hardly heard the remark. Her hand had touched a paper at the bottom of the sack. It proved to be one of the stock certificates to which was attached a note:

> "Jacques:
>   Made a neat deal on the earrings. Send Bunny Reynolds a dividend to keep her from hollering when she finds out.
>
>   Sid"

"This is all we need," said Nancy, rising. "Ned, will you come to police headquarters with me?"

"You bet. I drove your car over here this morning."

It took only half an hour to get there. Nancy handed the bag of mink peltries over to Chief Wester at once and explained what it held.

"Fine work, Miss Drew," he said, as he shook hands with her. The chief suggested that she go into his office for the interview with the prisoners, and that Ned wait for the right moment to bring in the loot.

"I got in touch with Mrs. Packer and the Mason-ville police," the chief went on, as he closed the outer office door. "They both confirm what you told us about Mitzi Channing." He called to a guard to bring in the prisoners through the rear office door.

Upon seeing Nancy, the Channings and Dun-stan Lake looked at one another nervously.

"Miss Nancy Drew is here to identify you men as her abductors last night," the chief said. "What have you to say for yourselves?"

"Not a thing," Channing managed to say in a tense voice. "I never saw her before."

"Me neither," Dunstan Lake added, moistening his dry lips.

"What about you, Mrs. Channing?" the officer asked.

"I could say a great deal about that meddlesome little sleuth," Mitzi snapped, glaring at Nancy. "As for your outrageous charges, we deny every one of them."

"Miss Drew has just brought something that may refresh your memories," Captain Wester said coldly.

He flung open the front office door. "Mr. Ned Nickerson, will you come in, please?" he called.

The chief took the pouch from Ned's hands and laid it on his desk. The prisoners stared in stunned silence.

"The evidence in here is enough to convict you," Wester said. "Nancy Drew saw you put this bag in the snow statue not long after the peltries were stolen, Channing, or Jacques Fremont, which I believe is the name you use in Canada."

To Nancy's surprise, it was Mitzi who broke down first. Sobbing, she advised the men to admit their part in the racket.

"It'll go easier with us," she said. "But someday I'll get even with you, Nancy Drew, for what you've done."

The men finally confessed. Lake was the leader and had thought up the idea of stealing the furs from the various ranches and secreting them in the snow statue while going for another haul.

"Ned and I must be going, Chief Wester," said Nancy. "Only I'd like to ask Mr. Channing a question first." Turning to the dejected prisoner, she inquired, "Did you send me a telegram and sign my father's name to it?"

"Yes. You were always on our trail and we wanted to get rid of you until we could make our haul and escape. We hoped to catch you alone on your way to the hotel before you phoned your father."

"And one of you was eavesdropping at my aunt's cottage to find out if I were going to the inn?"

"I was," Dunstan Lake admitted, as the prisoners were taken away.

The chief thanked Nancy again, then she and Ned started for Aunt Lou's cottage.

"I guess this ends *The Mystery at the Ski Jump*," Ned remarked, as he turned into the camp lane. "It was exciting, but I'll be glad to just sit and talk to you awhile. In two days the old grind at Emerson begins again. Nancy, don't you dare get involved in another mystery before the winter carnival at Emerson."

"I promise," the young detective replied laughingly, but secretly hoped another mystery would turn up very soon.

It did indeed, and came to be known as *The Secret of the Velvet Mask*.

Nancy and Ned had barely stepped inside the cottage when George cried, "Look! Someone's coming in a car. Could it be John Horn?"

"Not in a car." Bess giggled.

Their visitor was not the old trapper but Mr. Drew. He and Nancy embraced joyfully.

"When Aunt Lou telephoned me you were lost, Nancy," the lawyer said, "I took the first plane I could get. Poor Hannah was frantic too."

"Have you told her I'm all right?" Nancy asked.

"Yes. I phoned her from the inn. She was certainly relieved. And Hannah sent you a message, Nancy. Mitzi's skating partner Smith and that printer Ben in New York who put out the

Forest Fur Company stock have been arrested."

"Serves him right!" George stated firmly.

"And by the way," Mr. Drew went on, "while I was at Longview, I talked to Chuck. John Horn came in too. You'll all be pleased to know that, with the old trapper's sworn testimony, Chuck is sure to regain most of his inheritance. His uncle had put the money into his own bank account, but fortunately hadn't spent much of it."

Then Mr. Drew smiled at his daughter. "Chuck asked me to deliver a message. He thinks the successful outcome of his case and Nancy's calls for a celebration. He's inviting all of you to be his guests at dinner at Longview tomorrow night."

"Hurrah!" Bess shouted. "A party!"

Next morning Mr. Drew was obliged to return to River Heights. The young people spent the day enjoying winter sports, then cast aside ski suits and boots for party clothes.

When they arrived at the inn they found that Chuck had engaged a small, private dining room where places were set for ten persons. John Horn and Mr. Wells were to join the party. There were colorful favors at each plate and a special menu, with the promise of dancing afterward. When dessert was brought in, their host rose from his chair.

"This is a happy occasion for me," Chuck announced. "I've not only had gratifying news from my lawyer, Mr. Drew, but I've made some grand, new friends, among them one of the world's cleverest detectives."

Nancy found herself blushing as the others applauded.

"I've been given the pleasure of making some presentations. Mrs. Packer has asked the police to present her diamond earrings and the pin to Nancy because of the clever way in which she tracked down the thief. And here they are!"

"Oh, Nancy, they're beautiful!" gasped Bess, as Nancy accepted the sparkling jewelry.

"B-but I don't deserve these," the embarrassed girl protested.

"Indeed you do." Chuck smiled. "You deserve them—and more."

As he spoke, the ski instructor laid a gaily wrapped box on the table before Nancy. "This," he told her, "is from Mr. Wells, John Horn, and me."

There was a great hush as Nancy lifted the box lid. Inside were several glossy mink peltries— enough to make a lovely scarf.

Nancy's eyes were moist with emotion. She did manage to thank them all, and say she would wear the lovely neckpiece in remembrance of her adventure at Big Hill.

As the young people arose to attend the dance,

Mr. Wells called Ned, Burt, and Dave aside. There was a howl of laughter. Then Ned came walking forward with a deer head held in front of his face.

"For our fraternity house, girls. The old dear invites you to come to Emerson and help hang him over the fireplace!"